HARMONY ISLAND GAZETTE

SWEET TEA AND A SOUTHERN GENTLEMAN
BOOK 5

ANNE-MARIE MEYER

To all the readers who think they found their very own knight in shining armor, only to discover he's really the villain... may I suggest the monster?

Author Warning:

This book deals with physical abuse and it is shown on page. If that is something you are sensitive to, perhaps skip this book (or avoid chapter 23).

ANNE-MARIE

PROLOGUE

SWEET TEA &
SOUTHERN GENTLEMAN

Boone

"Ladies and Gentleman, I would like to welcome you to Richmond International airport. The local time is now 6:35. We're coming into gate B7. If you have a connecting flight, please check the monitors. If this is your final destination, welcome home."

My entire body tensed at the last few words before the stewardess went into the credit card speech she'd given earlier in the flight.

Home.

That word was like a dagger to my heart.

I pulled my hat further down as I stared out the window, watching the plane taxi its way to the gate. My stomach knotted the closer we got. I didn't want to be here. I didn't want to be discharged.

When my commanding officer walked into the doctor's office after she diagnosed me with permanent hearing loss in my left ear, I'd wanted to bolt from the room. The military was my home. That was where I was meant to be. Returning to civilian life wasn't in the cards for me.

Mom was gone. I had no other family. The guys I served with were my people. I wasn't supposed to ever leave.

But here I was, dressed in a t-shirt and jeans. The only remnants of my military service were the dog tags around my neck and the green bag I'd shoved all my items into before I walked away from the only family I had left.

Here, I was alone. And I hated being alone.

I waited until the plane was empty before I grabbed my backpack from under the seat in front of me, used the headrest to pull my body to standing, and shuffled into the aisle.

The two stewardesses who had worked the flight watched me as I passed by. I pulled my hat further down on my head as I nodded at them.

"Thank you for your service," one said.

My entire body stiffened at her words. I glanced over my shoulder and met her gaze before I just nodded and left.

She didn't know what she was saying. I joined the service to redeem myself. I'd failed to save my mother's life, and I'd vowed that I was never going to make that mistake again.

Now, I didn't know what I was going to do.

I walked through the airport at a brisk pace. I didn't want any more civilians thanking me for my service. Plus, being around this many people made me anxious. By the time I got to the luggage carousel, I breathed a sigh of relief. The suitcases and bags were already out and circling around.

I found my green bag, grabbed the handle, and swung it up onto my shoulder. I saw an older man wearing a Vietnam vet hat. He nodded in my direction, and I returned the gesture but didn't stop to speak to him. Instead, I just ducked my head and hurried away.

As I walked to the sliding doors, I grabbed out my phone and opened the rideshare app I'd downloaded last time we were stateside and we'd wound up barhopping. I was grateful for it now as I scanned through the cars that were parked and ready.

I selected the simplest one I could find and reserved it as I walked out onto the sidewalk. It didn't take me long to find the white Toyota Corolla. I knocked on the trunk and it opened. I dumped my bag into the back before slamming the trunk closed and pulling open the left rear door.

"Good evening," The driver said from over his shoulder. The man looked old enough to be my father.

I just nodded.

"Where are we going tonight?"

"To get my truck." The Ford F-250 had been a gift from my uncle, my mom told me. I never knew if that was true or not. I'd never met the man. But I loved the truck. It was the only sentimental piece I kept stateside for when I was on leave.

The man nodded and took off through the throng of cars and people. I settled back in my seat and closed my eyes. I wanted to nap—I was exhausted—but I couldn't.

Not when I knew where I was headed after getting my truck.

It had been a long time since I'd come back to Harmony Island, North Carolina. I'd written off the place a long time ago. Once Mom was in the ground, I left and never looked back. Her house, her things. They sat untouched. Now, the city of Harmony was forcing my hand. I needed to decide what I was going to do with the house or they were going to make the decision for me.

As soon as I got to my truck, I'd fill the tank with gas and take off down the highway to North Carolina whether I wanted to or not.

It was a thirty-minute drive from the airport to the storage facility where I'd left my truck. I paid the driver and opened the door, not wanting to engage in niceties. I moved to tap the trunk, but the driver beat me to it. The trunk swung open, and I reached in to grab my bag. I swung it up onto my shoulder, slammed the truck closed, and headed inside to the lobby.

A woman who looked no older than twenty was sitting behind the registers, snapping her gum and staring at her phone. When the bells on the door jingled, she glanced up at me from over her glasses.

"How can I help you?" she asked as she rested her hands on the counter in front of her but didn't let go of her phone.

"I'm here to pick up my truck." I pulled my wallet from my back pocket and fished out the ticket they'd given me when I'd left it.

She sighed as she set her phone down and took the ticket from me. She typed a few things into the computer in front of her and then nodded as she turned to the small cabinet that held a bunch of keys on hooks. "Wait out front, and I'll bring it around. Johnny was working on it earlier this week. It should be good to go."

I was so grateful when I found this place. Not only did they store vehicles, they did regular checks to make sure fluids didn't go bad and that the truck would still start.

"Thanks," I said as I tapped the counter.

She murmured a quick, "uh huh," as she disappeared through the back door.

I made my way back to the front. I took a deep breath of the evening air and tipped my face up. The sun was now tucked behind the trees, and darkness was slowly creeping around me. I knew once I got into my truck I would feel better. I would feel more like me than I had in a while.

The familiar sight of my black truck rounding the corner of the building brought a smile to my lips. She looked good. Johnny had kept his promise to keep her in pristine condition. Johnny gave me the cursory finger raise from the steering wheel as he pulled up next to me. I waited while he pulled open the driver's door and hopped down.

"Hey, man," he said. He was tall with a deep, gravelly

voice, and he wore a trucker hat. His hands were stained, no doubt from car fluids.

"Thanks for taking care of her," I said as I shook his extended hand.

"My pleasure." He stepped to the side so I could get a full view of the inside of my truck.

"Candice will settle your account."

"Perfect." I swung my bag into the back of the cab. Then I climbed into my truck. I pulled the door closed, but Johnny looked like he wanted to say something, so I rolled the window down.

He tapped the door with his hand and smiled up at me. "Thanks for your service."

My throat tightened, and my smile faded. I knew he meant well, but I wasn't sure if I was going to survive civilian life if this was what I was going to face every time I got around people. "Sure," I said before I put my truck into drive and rolled forward.

I didn't look back as I pulled out of the parking lot and onto the highway. I kept the window down, enjoying the cold night air rushing around me as I raced down the road. I leaned forward and flipped on the radio, blaring a country station.

I didn't stop until I crossed the state line into North Carolina. I had a few more hours until I got to Harmony, so I stopped at a gas station. I filled up on gas, used the bathroom, and grabbed an energy drink to help keep me awake.

It was eleven before I pulled into the outskirts of

Harmony Island. It felt both familiar and foreign at the same time. I had some memories of this place, but not enough to feel nostalgic. If anything, this place represented a time in my life that I wanted to forget.

I pulled down a side street and idled as I got out my phone and found the email from Harmony City Hall. I could picture my mother's home, but I couldn't remember how to get there. I punched her address into my map app and waited for the familiar computer voice to tell me where to go.

Ten minutes later, I was sitting in front of her house in the small community complex of Harmony Cove. Mom's house was small compared to the others around it. The grass was long and danced in the night breeze. The windows were dark, and I felt stupid for wanting a light to go on. A sign of life that I knew was no longer there.

I dropped my gaze to my lap and cursed under my breath. I was weak. And weakness was what put me in this situation in the first place. If only I'd been stronger, she might still be here.

Guilt and anger rose up inside of me. I gripped the steering wheel so tight that my knuckles turned white. No longer able to sit in front of the physical representation of all my failures, I threw my truck into drive and sped away.

I needed a drink.

Harmony Pub came up when I searched local bars while I waited for the light to turn green. It only took seven minutes before I was pulling into a vacant spot near the back of the parking lot. I turned my truck engine off and pulled the keys from the ignition before yanking open my door and climbing out.

The gravel crunched under my feet as I made my way to the front door. Harmony Pub was buzzing with conversation, the jukebox in the corner, and a friendly game of darts happening in the back.

I pulled my hat down to cover my face as I approached the bar. I doubted that anyone would recognize me. My mother kept to herself when she lived here, and I was back and forth so much that I hadn't made any concrete relationships. All I wanted to do tonight was drink—not engage in awkward small talk.

I found a barstool in the corner and settled down. The bartender caught my gaze and raised his eyebrows while he filled a glass.

"Whiskey," I said, and he nodded in acknowledgement.

I set my phone face down on the bar and settled back in my seat. I wasn't sure where I was going to spend the night. If I had to, I'd stay the night in the bed of my truck. God knows, I'd slept in worse places.

"I don't know what to tell you, Rich. I really don't know of anyone who could help you out," the bartender said as he set the tumbler of whiskey down in front of me. He had his attention on an older man who was standing a few feet away from me. He didn't look like he was drinking. His expression was desperate as he glanced around.

"Jax, I'm desperate," Rich said.

The bartender hadn't stepped away from me. Instead, he just folded his arms as he leaned against the counter. "I get that, I just don't know of any *bodyguard*." He flinched like saying that word felt weird. Then his gaze drifted over to me. He frowned. "Are you new around here?"

I glanced from Jax to Rich, who had approached me. I stiffened. I didn't like it when people approached me, especially when I didn't know who they were.

"I'm passing through," I said, hoping my short answer wouldn't invite more questions.

Jax nodded, his gaze dropping to the tattoo on my arm. "You military?"

"Honorably discharged," I muttered under my breath, hating every syllable.

"Huh." Jax flicked his gaze from me to Rich. "Maybe..." He paused as he extended his hand in my direction as if inviting me to provide my name.

"Boone," I said before I could stop myself. *Shit.* Realizing I'd just put myself squarely into this conversation with these strangers, I turned to Rich. "What are you looking for?"

Rich met my gaze, and I could see the desperation in his gaze as he studied me. "I need someone to protect my daughter from her abusive husband."

The bar around me faded away. Anger rose up inside of me as I leaned toward him and said, "Tell me more."

1

JUNIPER

Two pink lines.

I stared down at the pregnancy test that was resting on the edge of the bathroom sink in front of me. I blinked once. Twice. Three times.

No matter how many times my eyes had to refocus, those two pink lines remained.

I was pregnant.

My stomach twisted and turned. I clutched my middle and doubled over as my knees began to give out. I knew I should catch myself, but my brain wasn't connecting with the rest of my body, and the ground was coming toward me at a rapid pace.

"Whoa, whoa," Boone's smooth, deep voice rang in my ears as I felt his arms surround me. He went with me as he lowered me to the floor.

Once I was sitting on the ground, he let go but remained crouched down next to me.

I closed my eyes and tipped my head back, resting it on the wall. My head was spinning with questions and I couldn't seem to focus on anything.

"What am I going to do?" I finally whispered. I shook my head slightly from side to side.

"Are you disappointed?" Boone asked after a few seconds of silence.

A flutter of excitement danced in my stomach as I digested his question. Truth was, I'd always wanted to be a mother. I always thought that Kevin and I would have tons of babies and grow old together with our family around us. That was before Kevin informed me that having children was not in his life plan.

He was never going to be a father. Therefore, *I* was never going to be a mother.

Back then, I'd convinced myself that, eventually, he'd change his mind. We were still young. Sure, Kevin was determined to grow his advertising business, but aging had a way of slowing people down and causing them to take stock of their life. I just needed to wait until having a family became a priority for him like it was for me.

What a fool I'd been.

I peeked over at Boone. He was sitting next to me now. He'd hooked one arm around the knee that he'd brought up to his chest, and he was staring at the ground in front of him.

It was nice having him here with me. I wasn't sure what

I would have done if I'd learned this information on my own. Even though I knew nothing about this man, it was nice that he was sitting here with me. Heaven knows, he didn't have to.

Realizing that I couldn't spend the day sitting on the disgusting bathroom floor, I shifted my weight so I could stand. "We should probably get back," I said as I placed my hand down on the ground next to me to support my body.

Boone was faster than I was, and suddenly, he was standing and had his hands wrapped around my other arm to help me up. I was on my feet in record time. Once he was certain that I was stable, he let me go and took a step back, keeping his gaze focused on me like he was still uncertain if I was stable enough to remain upright on my own.

"Thanks," I whispered as I brushed the front of my pants. He raised his eyebrows as if to ask me why I was thanking him. My cheeks heated as I hurried to add, "For helping me up, getting the test, waiting with me..." I offered him a small smile. "For everything."

Boone flicked his gaze up at the pregnancy test still resting on the sink before bringing it back to settle on me. "You're welcome."

I held his gaze for a few seconds before I took in a deep breath and turned back to the sink to pick up the test and the empty box. I buried them deep under the used paper towels in the trash can. With that now taken care of, I returned to the sink and flipped the water on. I slathered up my hands, and once they were rinsed, I moved to grab some paper towels to dry off.

Boone was at the sink, washing his hands. By the time I'd tossed the wadded up paper towels into the trash, he was finished and pulling some from the dispenser. I watched him, wondering what he thought about this.

I was fairly certain that this hadn't been a part of whatever deal my dad had made with him. After all, sitting on the bathroom floor while I had a freakout over a positive pregnancy test didn't seem like something my father would ask him to do. I needed to make sure that what happened here would stay between us. Even though he worked for my dad, I needed him to keep this a secret.

"Can we keep this between us?" The words tumbled from my lips before I could police them.

Boone stopped drying his hands and glanced over at me. He studied me for a moment before he nodded. "Of course."

Relief flooded my body. "Good." I sucked in my breath. "I just...I'm just not ready..." I pinched my lips together as the reality of my situation came crashing down around me. I was going to have to tell my parents. I was going to have to tell Kevin. His family was going to find out.

My plan to permanently cut Kevin and the whole Proctor family from my life had evaporated with the appearance of those two pink lines. My world began to spin around me once more, so I slammed my eyes shut in an effort to gain some control.

"You don't have to justify to me how you want to

handle this. I'll keep your secret as long as you want me to."
Boone's voice seemed closer. I opened my eyes to see that
he was standing in front of me now. His gaze was sharp and
direct, like he wanted me to know that he meant what he
said.

I held his gaze before I slowly nodded. "Thanks," I
whispered.

His jaw muscles twitched before he nodded, stepped
back, and tossed the paper towels into the garbage. Then he
grabbed the bathroom door handle and turned it. He held
the door open and stepped to the side so I could pass
through.

I nodded my thanks to him, but just as I stepped outside,
I stopped. Mom was standing there with her arms crossed
and her eyes narrowed. I startled, grabbing my heart as I
yelped and stumbled back.

"Geez, Mom," I said as I bent forward to catch my
breath.

"What were you two doing in the bathroom?" Mom
asked as her gaze slowly shifted from me to Boone, who was
still holding the door. He looked like a deer in headlights.

Not wanting him to get in trouble for me, I straightened
and forced a smile. "I was having Boone check out a mole
that looks cancerous."

Mom snapped her gaze to me. "Don't be crude," she
scolded.

I sighed loud enough for her to hear. "Listen, the toilet
was clogged, and I was struggling to get it clear. Boone was

kind enough to help me." I raised my eyebrows as I stared at her. "I can ask you next time, though."

Mom pursed her lips and shook her head. "No, no. That's okay." She smiled at Boone. "Thank you for saving my daughter. You know, I always tell her to eat fiber, but she never listens."

"Ma!"

Boone had left the bathroom door and was a few steps away. The door latch clicked behind me. "It's okay, Mrs. Godwin," Boone said as he smiled down at her. "I was happy to help."

Before I could correct Mom that I wasn't the one who clogged the toilet, Boone was out of earshot. Mom called another thank-you after him before she turned to look at me.

"Mother," I said with my eyes wide so she could feel the weight of my frustration.

"What?" she asked.

"I wasn't the one who clogged the toilet." My face felt fiery hot as embarrassment coursed through me.

She frowned. "I thought you said—"

"It was a customer."

Her eyes widened as her lips formed an "o." Then she paused and shrugged. "Honest mistake."

"No. That's not an honest mistake." I closed my eyes, praying that Boone hadn't picked up on what my mother had insinuated. "And why did you say that I don't eat enough fiber? I'm a grown woman. I can take care of myself." To my mother, I must still be this little girl who was too scared to use the bathroom because she was worried what might come crawling up from the sewers.

"When you were a kid—"

"Ugh, Mom."

She just shrugged. "History has a way of repeating itself."

I shook my head. "I'm ending this conversation right now." I studied her for a moment before I let out an exasperated sigh and turned to leave.

"You shouldn't be embarrassed. Everyone does it!" Mom called after me.

My cheeks were on fire as I hurried away from her. I ran down a few aisles before I stopped to take in a few deep breaths.

I contemplated trying to find Boone to explain, but I realized that probably would not help. It was best to leave it in the past and move forward. Plus, I had much bigger things to worry about right now, namely, the baby growing in my belly and how I was going to tell its father.

Kevin had to know, and I had no idea how I was going to tell him.

Or how he was going to respond.

2

BOONE

SWEET TEA &
SOUTHERN GENTLEMAN

Nine o'clock came too fast. I was restocking the prepackaged lunch meat when Mr. Godwin walked by and announced that it was closing time and he was locking the doors. I nodded at him to acknowledge that I'd heard. And the reality of what waited for me when I walked out of the store hit me like an anvil to the head.

I knew at some point I was going to have to go to Mom's house. I was going to have to face my past and the demons that lived there. But I wasn't ready. And I hated that the anxiety of that decision reignited inside of me every evening. I could only hope that Mr. Godwin wanted me to stay the night again. Then the decision would be made for me.

I just wondered if Juniper would fight him about it like she had the first night. After this morning in the bathroom, I felt a shift in our relationship. I was more than happy to give her space, but she seemed to need me. And it felt good to focus on someone else's problems rather than my own.

It was the reason I'd joined the service. I couldn't save Mom, but I could save others. In some messed up, Rorschach-test way, saving others filled the void created inside of me as a child. Watching my mother get tossed around by every guy she brought home had left me feeling helpless.

I didn't know a lot Juniper's story, but I knew one thing —her husband was an asshole. What kind of guy would treat her like that? He didn't deserve Juniper. She deserved better than him.

I flexed my hand before I reached into the cardboard box and pulled out some packages of lunch meat. When I saw him grab her hand at the diner yesterday, it took all my strength not to pull him up and take him outside. There were very few things that could get my blood boiling, and lowlifes who abused women were one of them.

Whenever I saw a man lord himself over a woman, like Juniper's husband had, it made me lose all the self-control that I'd worked so hard to harness. I didn't think, I acted. I wasn't surprised by Juniper's response. I'd seen it before as a kid. Mom's blank stare as she tried to process what was happening to her. She was mentally calculating what defying him would do to her situation in the future. Women in battered relationships never stayed because they wanted to.

They knew where acting out left them. If they weren't ready to face that consequence, then they stayed passive and subservient. Relationships were a game of chess, and they were weighing whether sacrificing their queen was the right move or not.

Many people saw women like that as weak, but Juniper wasn't weak. The tongue-lashing she'd given me after he left had proven that. She had feelings and opinions—she just lost that part of herself when he was around. And that thought had me flexing my hand as I stood next to the fridge. The desire to take care of her ex grew stronger. If she wasn't going to leave him, I could make him disappear and make it look like an accident.

It's not like I had anything to lose.

"You okay, Boone?" The soft, feminine voice of Mrs. Godwin pulled me from my thoughts. I blinked and turned to face her. "What?" I asked as my sight cleared and I saw her standing in front of me with her eyes wide.

"You're manhandling the meat," she said, nodding toward my hands.

I glanced down to see that my knuckles were white as I was practically strangling the food. I quickly relaxed my fingers and set the lunch meat down onto the cart that was empty, except for the cardboard box I was currently unpacking.

"Yeah, sorry," I said as I forced thoughts of Juniper and her husband from my mind and smiled at her. "I just got lost in thought, I guess."

Mrs. Godwin brought her gaze up to meet mine. "Ah." She flicked her gaze down to my hands and then to the clipboard she was holding in her hand. "Mr. Godwin was wondering what your availability was for the week so I can make the schedule."

I turned to the fridge and tucked the slightly strangled lunch meat behind the other packages I'd unloaded earlier. "I'm completely free," I said as I turned back around to grab the remaining three packages.

"Completely free?" she asked.

I nodded. "Whatever you need, I can do." When she didn't respond right away, I glanced over at her. "Is that okay?"

She was writing something on her clipboard, but I could tell that her eyes were brimming with tears. "God truly blessed us when he sent you here."

I frowned, not expecting her to say that. She flourished her pen like she had just finished off her sentence with a period and glanced up at me. She sniffled, and I knew that I couldn't let her walk away until I asked if everything was okay. "Mrs. Godwin—"

"Betty."

I blinked. My momma had raised me to be a good southern boy. You never called a lady by her first name. "Miss Betty."

She gave me an exasperated look before she nodded. "Yes?"

"Is everything okay?"

She tucked the clipboard under her arm so she could pinch the bridge of her nose. She closed her eyes, and I watched as her shoulders rose and fell with each breath. "I'm just worried."

"Anything I can do to help?"

She pulled her hand away from her nose and glanced up at me. "You're already helping more than you know." She smiled. "Your help with Juni and around the store...has been a blessing."

"Of course."

She studied me as if she were weighing her words carefully. Then I saw something shift in her gaze. Like she had made a decision. "I got a call from my sister this morning. She lives in California."

"Okay."

She glanced around her. "She had an irregular mammogram." She paused. "A mammogram is where they take a woman's breast—"

"I know what a mammogram is," I said quickly. The earlier conversation with Mrs. Godwin and Juniper had taken a strange turn. I wasn't ready to relive that awkwardness all by myself. At least outside of the bathroom, I could leave Juniper to deal with her mom. There was no way I could leave Mrs. Godwin standing in the lunch meat section alone. My upbringing wouldn't allow me to leave her mid conversation.

Mrs. Godwin blinked. "Right. You have a mom." She

shook her head. "Anyway, I want to be there for my sister. But Rich...he won't leave Juni with Kevin in town. I was thinking that you might be able to..." She let her voice trial off as she tipped her face forward and raised her eyebrows.

I frowned, not wanting to misinterpret. "Do you want me to convince him to go?" I asked.

"Rich trusts you. If you tell him you've got everything covered, I'm sure he'll feel much better about leaving."

It was strange to me how trusting the Godwins were. To me, if a person was breathing, they could hurt you. Even the most kind and passive person could turn on a dime. So it was unnerving that these people would be so willing to leave their store and their daughter in the hands of a man they just met.

Sure, I had the backing of a few people in town. People that had grown up with my mom and had known me since I was a boy. But Betty and Rich didn't know much about me. It felt as if they were desperate to trust someone and I was their best option.

"If that's what Mr. Godwin really wants, I'm happy to help."

Betty's eyes glistened with tears once more as she smiled up at me. "Thank you, Boone. You're such a good guy."

I forced a smile even though her words didn't make me happy. If I was such a good guy, my mom might still be alive. If Mrs. Godwin only knew how much I'd failed the one woman who I should have protected, she might not say those words. But her eyes were so wide and her smile so big, all I could do was nod. "Thanks."

"Let me go see if I can find him," she said as she pulled out her clipboard and hurried away, flipping papers, before I could stop her.

I hadn't meant that I would talk to him right this moment. Mrs. Godwin was gone before I could say anything. I was left standing there, with lunch meat in both hands, staring at her retreating frame and wondering what I'd just gotten myself into.

I had just finished breaking down the box when Mr. Godwin stumbled toward me. He was protesting as Mrs. Godwin shoved him toward me.

"Lord, woman," he grumbled as he straightened up, rubbing his back. "Whatever Boone has to say to me, I can take my own time getting to him."

"We don't have a lot of time," she said as she followed behind him, waving her hand in my direction. "Talk to him."

Mrs. Godwin was sneaky. Suddenly, *I* was the one who had to convince Mr. Godwin to leave his business and daughter solidly in my hands. I straightened and set the box cutter down on the top of the cart.

"Alright, son," Mr. Godwin said as he squared his shoulders and stood in front of me. "What do you have to talk to me about so badly that my wife had to manhandle me to get me over here?"

Embarrassment coursed through me as heat pricked at my skin. I glanced over at Mrs. Godwin, who looked so hopeful as she studied me. I really was on my own. I sucked in my breath and turned back to look at Mr. Godwin.

"Sir," I started, and then every single word flew from my mind. How much did I say? How was I going to convince this man that he should take his wife away from his home and leave me in charge?

"Dad?" Juniper's voice broke up the silence. We turned to see her approaching us from the cereal aisle.

She frowned as she glanced between me and her parents. "What's going on here?" Her gaze lingered on me, and without thinking, I glanced over to Mrs. Godwin. Her eyebrows were so high, they looked as if they were going to disappear into her hair. Juniper seemed to pick up on it and turned her attention to her mom.

"Mother?" she asked. "What are you planning with Boone behind my back?" Her hands were on her hips.

Mrs. Godwin started sputtering. I could tell that she was flustered, and I felt bad for her. Her lips were moving but no sound was coming out. She kept glancing over at Mr. Godwin and then back to her daughter. I feared she would melt into a puddle on the floor, so I took a step toward them. "Mrs. Godwin was telling me how worried she was about her sister in California."

All gazes snapped to me. Juniper's eyes widened.

I swallowed and continued. "After her sister's irregular mammogram"—that word felt weird on my tongue—"she was wanting Mr. Godwin to come with her to help support the two of them through this." I paused. "Mr. Godwin would be there to help Mrs. Godwin, who is there to help her sister." I pointed to imaginary people in front of me as I explained, as if that was all it took to make this situation make sense.

Silence filled the space around us as my words lingered in the air. I waited for someone to speak, but no one seemed ready to. I feared what I was going to say if I kept going, so I just stood there, waiting for someone—preferably Mrs. Godwin—to pick up the baton.

"I think that's a great idea," Juniper said.

I wasn't the only one who was surprised she spoke first. We all turned to stare at her. She was studying the ground and nodding. When she looked up, she focused on her dad.

"I think you should go. I'm here. I can take over the store. Plus, with Katie, Sal, Jordan and Tom..." She paused and glanced up at me. "And Boone." Was it wrong that my chest swelled a bit at the sound of my name on her lips? "We'll hold the fort down. You should go be with Aunt Christi. She needs you guys, and Mom needs you, Dad."

I watched as Juniper's gaze settled on Mr. Godwin, whose expression was stoic. He wasn't really looking at anyone in particular. He stared off into the distance as if he were chewing on Juniper's words.

"What do you say, Rich?" Mrs. Godwin asked.

He glanced over at her and then sighed. "I don't like the idea of leaving the store, but if it's what you need, then we should go."

Mrs. Godwin's eyes filled with tears once more. She

crossed the space between her and Mr. Godwin and wrapped her arms around him. "Thank you," she whispered.

I suddenly felt like I was intruding on an intimate family moment. I took a step back and focused on the floor in front of me as I waited for them to break apart. Movement in front of me drew my attention up, and I met Juniper's gaze. She was studying me like she was trying to figure something out.

Like she was trying to figure *me* out.

Unsure of what I was supposed to do, I offered her a small smile. She blinked as if she hadn't realized she'd been staring at me and moved her focus to her parents, who had released each other and stepped back.

"Let's close up the store and head home," Mr. Godwin said as Mrs. Godwin nodded.

I didn't wait for Mr. Godwin to excuse me. I grabbed ahold of the cart began pushing it toward the back of the store. When I got to the swinging doors that led to the back room, I turned and backed through them.

Once I was alone, I straightened. I exhaled as I scrubbed my face with my hand before tipping my head back and staring up at the ceiling. Getting this involved with the Godwin family seemed the exact opposite of what I'd wanted to do when I got back to Harmony.

I hadn't meant to insert myself into a family and pretend like my life wasn't a complete disaster. I'd intended to come back and keep to myself. Now, I was not only keeping

Juniper's secret, I seemed to be Mrs. Godwin's confidant as well.

If only these people knew how badly I'd failed my own family, they wouldn't be so eager to let me into theirs. If they knew the real me, they'd stay as far away as possible.

I wasn't a good person. And it was only a matter of time before they pushed me out of their lives forever.

3

ELLA

SWEET TEA & SOUTHERN GENTLEMAN

I yawned and stretched before pressing my hand into my lower back and curving it out to relieve the tension that had built up there. I slipped off my blue-light blocking glasses and closed my eyes before pinching the bridge of my nose. Gloria wanted me to proof the articles for Sunday before I left, so I'd spent the last few hours staring at a computer screen. My eyes were tired.

Gloria had been weird to me all day. After she learned about my encounter with the mystery man this morning, she was acting as if I couldn't be trusted. Every time I walked into a room while she was talking to someone, she dropped her voice to a hush before she promptly ended the conversation.

My spidey sense was going haywire not only from what the mystery man had said, but *how* he'd said it. But I was willing to let her weird behavior pass. After all, Gloria was my boss. If something was off-limits, I was going to honor that. But her behavior just heightened my suspicion that things around this town weren't exactly what people thought they were.

If she wanted to throw me off a scent, she was failing miserably.

My phone chimed. I flipped it over and glanced down to see a text from Asher. I smiled as I swiped the screen.

Asher: Burning the midnight oil?

I laughed and nodded as I picked up my phone to respond.

Me: Ding, ding, ding! We have a winner.

I pushed my chair back, stretching out my legs in front of me. I leaned back and let my muscles relax as I waited for Asher to respond.

Asher: Red looks good on you.

I frowned as I read his text. Then I glanced down at the red satin button-down shirt and black pencil skirt I was wearing. How did he...? I glanced around. Could he see me?

Asher: To the left

I glanced over to the wall on my left.

Asher: Other left

I glanced to the widow on my right and laughed. Asher was standing at my window with a coffee cup in each hand and a giant grin on his lips. He wiggled his eyebrows, and I shook my head as I moved to stand.

"Wanna let me in?" he shouted through the glass,

nodding toward the front door Gloria had locked when she left earlier that evening.

"You're such a dork." I stood and made my way through my office to the front room. Asher was standing at the door when I unlocked it and pushed it open. He instantly held out a cup of what I could only assume was my regular order, so I took it from him. "Thanks," I said as I held the cup in both hands and took a long sip. "You are a hero."

"That's me. Harmony's realtor by day, and coffee bringer by night," he said as he grinned at me.

I turned and moved away from the door so he could join me inside. He shut the door behind him and then glanced over at me. "Gloria's got you slaving away, huh?" he asked as he slipped his free hand into his front pocket and glanced around before taking a sip of his own coffee.

"Yeah. She wanted me to get the articles proofed before we send them to the printers on Sunday." I took another long drink, feeling better with each sip. "I was the one who volunteered to stay late."

He paused and looked at me. "You volunteered, or you *were* volunteered?"

I pursed my lips and raised my eyebrows as if to say, *what do you think?*

He tsked. "What did you do to tick Gloria off this time?"

I sighed and took a sip of coffee. I wasn't sure how much I wanted to tell him. Should I tell him about what happened when I got to work that morning? Or should I just let it go? Gloria told me not to do anything about what the man had said. The Proctors were rich. They had a lot of enemies in the community. The person was probably a spiteful individual who was just looking for revenge. There was no need to bite the hand that feeds you just because of baseless accusations.

And while I agreed with that, not looking into the accusations seemed strange as well. After all, that was the job of a journalist. It was my job to make sure that truths were revealed for the greater good. Ignoring something out of fear of whom it might upset went against everything I'd sworn to do when I decided to major in journalism. And then to have my editor—the woman who hired me to tell the truth—tell me not to so much as look into the family. It didn't sit right with me.

"Ella?"

Asher's voice brought me back to the present. I blinked and glanced over at him. He raised his eyebrows and was studying me like he was waiting for me to respond.

"I'm sorry, what?" I asked, forcing the thoughts of the mystery person into the locked box in the back of my mind. I wasn't going to worry about that right now.

"I asked you what you did to tick Gloria off."

I nodded. "Right." Then I shrugged. "Who knows why Gloria gets in the ruts she does."

Asher took another sip. "True." Then he glanced over at me. "I'm sorry. I didn't know that you'd be working under someone like her when I suggested that you come to Harmony." He sucked in his breath. "I guess I was just selfish, and I wanted you here."

I offered him a smile. "It isn't your fault. You didn't know." I took a few steps toward him and punched him playfully in the shoulder. "And I'm glad you told me about this job. I needed to get out of Chicago. Plus, I like Harmony. It's growing on me."

He looked relieved. "Good."

I nodded toward my office. "Wanna wait while I get the last article read, and then we can get some dinner?"

He studied me for a moment, his expression turning serious. "Does a bear poop in the woods?"

I laughed before shaking my head. I waved for him to follow me to my office. I sat at my desk, reading Sabrina's article about the Founder's Day Festival that was coming up. Asher sat in the chair across from my desk, doing work on his phone.

Needing to rest my eyes for a moment, I glanced up at him. His dark blond hair was sticking up, indicating that he'd just pushed his hand through it. His gaze was trained on his screen, and from the way his eyes were moving back and forth, he was reading something.

We'd met in college when we were both RA's. Our friendship had always been easy. We remained best friends until he moved away from Chicago after graduation and I stayed. I thought our relationship was over, but surprisingly, it didn't skip a beat. It just changed from seeing each other every day to texting or calling with a weekend get-together every few months.

When I told him that I'd just broken up with Scott, my long-term boyfriend, he told me about the job opening in Harmony. Chicago was a big city, but every corner I turned reminded me of Scott and the life I'd thought we were going to live. Moving away to a small southern town where my best friend lived seemed like just the escape I needed. So, I jumped on it despite my friends and family thinking I was crazy to do so.

As soon as I got here, Asher was there to help me. He found me a place to live and even showed up with groceries my first night. Even now, a few months later, he was bringing me coffee and keeping me company.

I was lucky to have such a good and loyal friend.

As if he had sensed my gaze, he glanced up at me and furrowed his brow. "What?"

I shrugged as I smiled. "Just thinking about how great of a friend you are."

His smile faded for a moment before he shrugged. "Yeah, well don't tell anyone. I've got an image to uphold here."

I laughed. "Oh, really?"

"Plus, my vetting process is long. I'm not sure many would get through it."

I leaned forward and rested my chin in my hand. "Is that so? I got through it."

He waved his hand in the air in front of him. "So, you know firsthand how ruthless I can be."

"Totally ruthless."

"I'm an animal."

I shook my head. "You're a dork."

He shrugged. "I am that as well. A ruthless, dorky animal."

I narrowed my eyes at him. "So...is this vetting process the reason why you're not dating anyone in Harmony?"

He paused before he looked over at me. "Since when did you start keeping tabs on my dating life?"

I leaned back in my office chair and bounced a few times. "It's hard to keep tabs on something that doesn't exist."

"Ouch. Shots fired, Calipso." Then he shrugged. "I haven't found the right girl. Plus, I'm working on building my company." He leaned forward. "Which is going magnificently, thank you for asking."

I raised my eyebrows. "Really?"

"Yep. I just got a call from Marcus Proctor. He's going to have some houses to list in the next month, and he wants me to be the agent for them." His smile was so wide that I hated how my stomach sunk at the mention of the Proctor patriarch. Was there a part of this town that family wasn't entrenched in?

"Wow. That's amazing," I said, hoping I sounded genuine in my excitement.

He nodded. "It's great for my company, especially since

I'm so new in a close-knit town. Having the backing of a big fish gains me trust that would have taken years to cultivate without it."

The reporter side of my brain kicked in. I knew I shouldn't pry, but this might be my chance to ask questions without arousing suspicion. If I was going to put this whole Proctor thing to bed, I needed to appease my gut feeling that there was more to the story than just a jilted friend. Something was going on in the Proctor family, and no one seemed willing to talk about it.

"Do the Proctors own a lot of real estate around here?" I brought my elbows up to rest them on the arm rests next to me.

Asher scoffed. "That's an understatement. They own a lot, and are quickly buying up properties to flip. With Deveraux construction investing heavily, the Proctors are on the fast track to own a huge portion of the town."

That in and of itself wasn't illegal. But it didn't sit right with me either. No family or entity should own that much of any town. Corruption had a way of rooting itself when competition was taken out.

"Oh no."

I glanced up to see Asher studying me. I frowned. "What?"

"I don't like that look on your face."

I reached up and squished my cheeks. "What look?"

He sighed as he sat back in his chair. "Your reporter

look." He raised his eyebrows. "It's the look you get when you're collecting information."

"Collecting information? Why would I be collecting information?" I lied.

He studied me. "Sometimes there's no story, El. Sometimes, what you see *is* what you get."

While I knew that was true, it was also false. There was always a story behind everything. Whether it was newspaper worthy or not, there was always a story behind everything a person did.

"I'm just curious," I said as I shrugged my shoulders and pushed around my computer mouse to wake up my monitor. "Can't I be curious?"

"You can be curious," Asher said.

"Good." Even though he'd agreed with me, I knew there was more he wanted to say. So, I paused to see if he was going to continue.

"It's just that this is a good thing for me. Having a relationship with the Proctors will really help take my business to the next level." He scrubbed his face. "I need this."

I gave him a soft smile. "I'm happy for you, Asher. I'm not trying to rain on your parade." That was true. I wanted only good things for my friend.

He studied me before he nodded. "I know. Thanks."

Silence fell between us, so I turned my attention to my monitor. "I have about five minutes until I'm done, and then we can head out. Does that work?" I asked, all the while not taking my eyes off the screen.

"That works," Asher said.

I forced my mind to focus on the words in front of me even though all it wanted to do was mull over my conversation with Asher. I was beginning to realize that if I acted on the suspicion that was growing in my gut, I was going to have to do it alone. My boss and my friend didn't seem interested in pulling on any thread that might unravel the Proctor family's secrets.

Sure, it might behoove me to forget what that man said to me this morning. The easy thing was to walk away and pretend it was just a figment of my imagination. Problem was, I wasn't the kind of girl who took the easy way out.

And I doubted that was going to change anytime soon.

4

JUNIPER

SWEET TEA & SOUTHERN GENTLEMAN

Monday morning, I was startled awake by the screeching sound of the alarm on my phone. I groaned and flipped to my side as I reached out to stop the obnoxious noise. Once silence surrounded me, I let out my breath and stared up at the dark ceiling.

Mom and Dad were leaving today to go help Aunt Christi, and I wanted to see them off.

I pulled off the covers and slipped my feet onto the floor. After grabbing my robe and opening my door, I padded down the hallway into the kitchen, where the light was on, causing me to squint as my eyes adjusted.

I yawned as I shuffled into the room and pulled out a chair that was tucked under the kitchen table. I pulled my robe tighter around my chest before reaching up to run my fingers through my tousled hair. Mom and Dad's larger luggage was sitting near the front door, but they were nowhere to be seen.

I glanced toward the living room, where I knew Boone had crashed the night before. After our family meeting at the store, Dad invited him over for dinner and then let him crash on the couch.

It was strange how, just a day ago, it had bothered me so much that he was staying with us, but now, it was nice. I liked that my parents trusted him. I was certain that if it had just been me suggesting they go spend some time in California, Dad would have never gone. I knew my father trusted me, but he worried too much about me and the store.

With Boone here, that worry seemed to have lessened.

I was grateful that they were leaving for an extended period of time. Kevin being in town and my pregnancy meant I was ready for some me time so I could process everything. And call me crazy, but I suspected Boone would be less nosy than my parents.

"Oh, good. You're up," Mom said as she hurried into the kitchen. She set her purse and larger carry-on down onto the table. Then she made her way over to the coffee machine and turned it on. "Think you can handle things here while we are gone?" she asked as she opened the cupboard and grabbed a mug.

"I think so," I said as I reached up and began massaging my temples. I loved my mom, and I knew she meant well, but I couldn't help but feel like her questions were steeped in disappointment.

"Listen, Juniper, I know you're still mad at me and Dad for bringing Boone on." She turned to face me. "But we're really just worried about you, and we want to make sure you are safe."

My gaze drifted back over to the living room before I focused back on Mom.

"I just hope someday you'll understand and forgive us for hiring him."

I raised my hand, hoping that was all it was going to take to stop my mom from continuing. Thankfully, she understood and pinched her lips together.

"Listen, Mom, it's okay. Boone is growing on me. Plus, it'll be nice to have some help while you're gone." I gave her a soft smile. "Go take care of Aunt Christi, and we'll take care of things here."

She studied me before she let out her breath. I could see the tears brimming in her eyes, so I pushed my hands against the table and stood. "Ma," I whispered as I crossed the space between us and pulled her into a hug.

She waved away my words but didn't fight me as I held her close. "I was just so worried about you, and now Christi."

"I know," I whispered, hating that I'd stressed my mother out this much. We didn't have the closest relationship, I had Kevin to thank for that. But I never wanted her to worry or stress out over me. Especially when she already had so much going on in her life. "I'll be fine."

She squeezed me tight before she let me go. The coffee

machine had finished filling her cup, so she stepped around me and grabbed it. I got a mug down from the cupboard and placed it under the coffee machine spout when I stopped.

Was coffee good for the baby?

My stomach churned as I realized that I didn't really know anything about being pregnant or what was going to happen to me. A wave of inferiority washed over me. I wasn't ready to be a mom yet. Not while my relationship with Kevin was so rocky. Not without a stable foundation to bring the baby home to.

I was going to have to tell Kevin...I was going to *have* to tell Kevin.

"Juniper, you okay?" Mom's voice pulled me from my thoughts as she appeared in my line of sight.

I blinked a few times willing myself to calm down. Once Mom and Dad were gone, I could freak out. Not before.

"Yeah, I'm fine," I whispered as I leaned against the counter next to me.

"You're as white as a ghost," she said.

My head was swimming and my ears felt clogged. I closed my eyes and folded my arms in an effort to give myself some deep, physical input.

"I don't think I ate enough yesterday," I mumbled.

"Juniper!" Mom's voice was one of exasperation and concern. "You need to be taking care of yourself." I heard the fridge open, but I didn't open my eyes to see what she was getting out. "Oh, Boone. I hope we didn't wake you up."

My body tensed at the sound of Boone's name. He was awake.

"Can you grab a chair and help Juniper? She's feeling lightheaded—hypoglycemic—because she didn't eat enough yesterday."

There was a quick sound of a chair being pulled out from the table, and then silence until, suddenly, I felt a hand on my arm and the warmth of Boone's chest as he bumped into my shoulder. I didn't fight him as he guided me over to the table. "The chair is behind you," he said, his voice low and smooth.

I kept my eyes slammed shut as I nodded and allowed him to help me onto the chair. I leaned forward, keeping my head down and my eyes closed tight as I took in deep breaths. I was going to have to get used to this nausea. If my pregnancy was anything like my mother's, I should clean the toilet today 'cause I was going to spend a lot of time next to it.

"Good lord, woman." Dad's voice was panicked. "Why are you making breakfast? We're going to be late to the airport if we don't leave now."

"Rich, your daughter is nauseous. I need to make her some eggs and toast."

I heard Dad's signature shuffle as he approached me.

"Morning, Boone," he said.

I tipped my head to the side. Was Boone still standing next to me? Why? The questions were forced from my mind with the feeling of Dad's hand on my shoulder.

"Are you sick, Juniper?"

I shook my head. "Just a little nauseous. Give me a piece of cheese and I should be fine," I said even though the thought of cheese made my stomach churn.

"See, Betty. She's fine. Let's go."

"I'm not leaving my daughter like this."

Dad grumbled like he always did when Mom put up a stink about something. "Boone," Dad bellowed.

"Yes, Mr. Godwin."

"Can you make breakfast?"

"Of course."

"Wonderful." I peeked over at them to see Dad clap Boone on the back. "You make Juniper some breakfast and get her feeling better while Betty and I meet the cab driver in the driveway."

Boone nodded before making his way over to the stove, where he awkwardly stood next to Mom, who was in the process of buttering up a pan.

"Betty, we have to go." Dad made his way toward her. I could see the panic in her gaze.

"I'll be fine, ma," I said, forcing my head upright and giving her a smile. I could tell that her reaction had a lot more to do with her fear of what she was going to find in California than her desire to take care of me. Sure, she was worried about me, but that was only a small part of her reaction. Once Mom got to Aunt Christi's, she'd feel better. She'd go into caretaker mode. But she needed an extra push to get her to take that first step.

Dad wrapped his arm around her shoulders and gently guided her from the kitchen. She sent one last glance back at me, and I smiled at her, hoping she'd feel encouraged instead of forced. She paused, and Dad whispered something to her. That seemed to do the trick, because she turned and made her way to the front door. Dad called for Boone to help with the luggage. Boone set the pan down on the stove before turning off the burner and grabbing the bags.

I nestled my forehead into the crook of my arm that was resting on the table and closed my eyes. I wasn't ready to tell my parents about the baby, but if I kept having nausea spells like this, they were going to get suspicious. Thankfully, with them leaving for a few weeks, I was going to have some time to come up with a game plan. I hoped that by the time they got back, I'd be feeling much better.

I wasn't sure how long I sat at the table with my eyes closed, but my ears pricked at the sound of the front door latching. Boone must be back. The sound of a pan being set on the stove to my left indicated that Boone was holding to the agreement he made with my mother that he would cook me some breakfast.

I must have dozed off. I felt a hand on my shoulder and snapped my eyes open, but my head felt cloudy as I straightened and glanced around. It took a moment for me to get my bearings. I glanced to the side to see Boone standing there with his eyes wide and a plate in his hand.

"Sorry," he murmured as he held up his free hand. "Didn't mean to wake you."

I wiped my mouth with the back of my hand. "I wasn't asleep," I said, but the grogginess in my voice said otherwise. And from the look on Boone's face, he didn't believe me. "Okay," he said as he set the plate down on the table.

My stomach grumbled at the sight of freshly scrambled eggs and buttered toast. I was ready to eat. Boone set a fork down next to the plate. A few seconds later, he handed me a glass of water. He stood awkwardly next to me, holding his own plate of food, as he glanced around.

I peeked over at him, wondering if he was waiting for me to give him permission to join me. Not wanting the silence between us to continue, I nodded toward the empty seat next to me. "I won't bite," I said around the eggs I was currently eating.

Boone hesitated but then pulled out the chair and sat down. We ate in silence together until my stomach was so full that I had to sit back just to give it more space. I folded my arms across my chest and shifted my gaze to Boone, who had just taken a bite of his toast. His focus was on the wall in front of him, so I took a moment to study him. I had so many questions about this man that I didn't know where to start.

"Thanks for making me some breakfast," I said as I reached forward and grabbed the glass of water before taking a sip.

Boone glanced over at me. His jaw muscles were moving as he chewed. He nodded. I waited a few seconds for him to finish chewing and swallow. He took a sip of coffee from his mug. "Of course."

Having had enough water, I set my glass back down. I wanted to ask him about his personal life, but I didn't know where to start. I didn't want to push him away before I could even get to know him.

He must have sensed that I was still staring at him because he flicked his gaze over at me a few times. "What?"

I tipped my head to the side. "Nothing..." I lied. I shifted in my chair before folding my arms across my chest once more. "It's just...never mind." Again, I couldn't quite piece together what I wanted to ask him. And I certainly didn't know how to ask it without coming across as nosy. I could hear my mother's voice, *Don't be prying into other people's business. It's not your row to hoe.* If she knew what I was fixing to do, she'd be so embarrassed.

Boone abandoned eating and was now sitting back in his seat, watching me. He had no intention of ignoring the fact that I'd been trying to say something, and he was going to wait for me to finish.

I met his gaze, and his eyes were dark as he studied me. He reached forward and took a sip of his coffee, all the while watching me from over the rim of his mug.

I sighed. I'd started opening Pandora's box, I might as well see it through. "What's in this for you?"

He frowned. "What do you mean?"

"I mean, this," I said as I pointed to my plate, myself, and the rest of the house in turn. "You're a grown man who looks like he's lived on his own for a long time. Why are you sleeping on my parents' couch and cooking me breakfast?"

My cheeks warmed with how direct my question was, but I needed to know. What was in it for him? "I mean, my parents aren't rich. So if you're hoping to get a payday"—I leaned forward—"it's not going to happen."

Boone didn't flinch as I got closer to him. In fact, he kept his gaze focused on me even though I'd just closed the space between us. He was so calm and unbothered that it was bothering me.

"Do you want free groceries?" I asked, narrowing my eyes. Then I shook my head. "You'll be disappointed to learn that my dad doesn't give out free food to me, and I'm his daughter. You don't have a prayer in hell..." I whispered, letting my voice trail off. "What is it you want from my family? From me?"

A silence fell between us as my last question lingered in the air. Boone's gaze was still locked with mine. There was a pain in his gaze that I'd never noticed. He was hiding something. But it wasn't just anything. It was something that had caused a wound big and deep.

I wondered if I should be worried. After all, I knew very little about this man. But instead of fear, a different feeling arose in my gut. It was the desire to heal whatever was haunting him.

Maybe it was because he was the only person on the planet who knew about the baby. Or the fact that he'd been there to support me through the last few traumatic things I'd gone through. But I cared. I cared enough to want to know more.

As if he suddenly realized that he was exposing more of himself than he wanted to, he blinked, pulled back, and returned to eating his eggs. After a few bites, he turned back to me. The storm had disappeared from his gaze.

"I don't want anything from you or your family. I just need a place to crash for a bit, and then I'll move on. That's it." He shrugged as he cut another chunk of eggs off with his fork and slipped it into his mouth.

I narrowed my eyes at him. If he noticed, he didn't acknowledge it. He couldn't possibly think I was going to buy that. I'd seen the pain he was carrying around. There was a mystery here, and I was going to solve it.

Maybe it had more to do with the fact that I wasn't ready to face my own demons—and focusing on Boone's was the perfect distraction—but I was going to find out why Boone was sleeping on my parents' couch. I was going to figure out why he got honorably discharged. And maybe I could lift some of the weight he seemed to be carrying around.

My problems were written in stone. I couldn't escape the inevitable. This baby was coming, forever tying me to Kevin and the Proctor family.

I couldn't imagine Boone having similar issues, which meant his problems had solutions. And I was going to spend all of my free time figuring out what those solutions were.

5

BOONE

SWEET TEA &
SOUTHERN GENTLEMAN

I cleaned up the kitchen after breakfast. Juniper offered to help, but I just shook my head and told her that I had it handled. She studied me, and I could tell that she was trying to size me up, but then she just shrugged and told me that she was going to take a shower. If I didn't want to clean everything, she'd finish what was left when she got out.

I nodded as I turned my focus to the dishes in the sink and waited for her to leave the room. Once she was gone, I felt like I could breathe.

It wasn't that I didn't want her around—I wanted her near me more than I should. There was just something in her that made me want to spill my guts. There was a depth to her gaze that both scared me and made me feel at home.

Maybe it was the secret she'd shared with me. I was pretty sure I was the only other human on Earth that knew her secret. It was intoxicating that she trusted me enough to let me in. I didn't realize it until now, but I had been craving a human connection, and Juniper had given it to me.

Now she was a drug that I didn't want to quit.

"You're an idiot," I whispered as I flipped the faucet on and watched the water pour over the dishes. I grabbed the dish soap and squirted a blue stream into the water. Suds appeared almost immediately.

I grabbed a dish cloth and plunged it into the water. My mind shut down as I washed each dish, rinsed it, and stacked it in the drying rack next to the sink. I didn't stop until I felt a hand on my shoulder. I startled and whipped around, flinging suds everywhere when Juniper came into view. She was standing there, her hair damp and her eyes wide.

"Boone, it's just me," she whispered as if she was trying to calm me down.

I forced my nerves to settle as I rolled my shoulders and cleared the fog that had settled in my brain. "Sorry," I said as I moved to grab the nearby dish towel to wipe my hands. "You startled me."

Her cheeks flushed. "Sorry." Then she motioned toward my phone, which I'd set on the counter before I started cooking breakfast. "Your phone was ringing. I thought maybe you were listening to something." Her gaze drifted to my ears.

I grabbed my phone and stuffed it into the back pocket of my jeans. "Thanks," I mumbled before I stepped around her and strode out of the kitchen. I didn't want her to ask me what I'd been thinking about so hard that I didn't hear my phone. I didn't want to stand there under her curious gaze. I didn't want her to get to know me.

I just wanted to hide.

I shut the bathroom door behind me. The sound of the door handle engaging echoed in the silence. I flipped the lock and then collapsed on the toilet seat, resting my elbows on my knees and dropping my head. I took in a few deep breaths as I tried to calm my body and my mind.

Not only had I slipped into a sort of trance while washing the dishes, but when Juniper touched me, my first instinct had been to react physically. Thankfully, the sight of her face as she stared up at me had been enough to pull me out of the haze that seemed to get thicker and thicker by the day. I feared what I might have done to her had I not bounced back so quickly.

I pulled my phone from my back pocket and stared at the black screen. How had I missed the sound of my phone ringing? That wasn't like me. I shook my head, trying to settle my thoughts that were pounding in my skull. I felt broken. And I was worried I would never get fixed.

I wasn't built for a quiet life in a small town. My childhood had been chaotic, and I had never settled down even when I was old enough to move on. My career in the military only exacerbated my need for action. There were never calm waters when you were a Navy SEAL.

To go from that to being alone with nothing to do in Harmony was eating away at me. Problem was, this black hole inside of me seemed to grow no matter how hard I tried to stop it.

I was a mess.

Unable to sit there, trying to dissect who I was and how I was going to fix my mountain of problems, I straightened and focused on my phone. I glanced down at the screen to see who had tried calling me. I didn't have friends, and my family was all gone. Perhaps, the reason I didn't hear my phone was because no one ever tried to call me on it.

The number wasn't in my contacts, but the caller did leave a message. I pressed the play button and turned on the speaker phone, causing a man's voice to fill the silent air.

"This message is for Mr. Lewis, the son of Hannah Lewis. This is Collin Baker. I am the property acquisitions manager for Proctor Realty." I sat up a little straighter at the mention of my mother's name. "We are interested in making an offer on your mother's property. We believe it's a handsome offer considering the state the house is in. We would also like to move fast, so if you could call me back at your earliest convenience, I would appreciate that."

He ended the message with a quick thanks and a goodbye. I sat there, staring at my phone screen. My thoughts were racing. To anyone else, this was just an innocent inquiry into my intentions with my mother's house. To me, this was a magnifying glass on my past and how I was going to handle everything that felt so broken.

I shook my head and stood, setting my phone down on the vanity and slipping off my shirt. I needed a hot shower to clear my head. Steam filled the bathroom as I waited for the water to warm. I stripped off the rest of my clothes and stepped under water hot enough to make my skin sting as it pelted me.

I rested my hands on the wall of the shower underneath the showerhead, and tipped my head forward, letting the water run down my face. I closed my eyes and took deep breaths in an effort to calm my mind. I knew I was going to have to face my mother's house someday. I just wasn't ready to do it today.

Fifteen minutes later, I was clean and felt a little more human. I dried off and then wrapped the towel around my waist as I stepped out of the shower and onto the plush bathmat.

I glanced around and cursed myself for showering without bringing in a change of clothes. I contemplated putting my dirty clothes back on but then glanced at the bathroom door. I doubted Juniper was still in the kitchen. From what I'd seen, she spent most of her time in her room.

And with Mr. and Mrs. Godwin gone, what would it hurt if I went out in a towel to quickly grab my clothes? I pushed my hand through my damp hair and forced my decision by unlocking the bathroom door and pulling it open.

I glanced down the hallway both ways to make sure I was alone before I stepped out and headed toward the living room, where my duffel bag was. Just as I neared the opening to the kitchen, Juniper appeared, walking straight into my bare chest.

My hands found her upper arms, but I was too late. Her soft hands sprawled across my chest. She made an adorable surprised yelp before her entire body stiffened.

It felt like an eternity before she peeked up at me, her eyes wide. "I'm so sorry," she whispered before she took a step back, breaking my hold. Her gaze flicked down to my chest before she returned it to mine as a blush emerged on her cheeks.

My body warmed under her scrutiny. For some reason, I wanted her to like what she saw. I knew I was not in a place in my life to let someone in, and I was certain she felt the same. "Sorry," I said, my voice low. I pushed my hand through my hair just for something to do instead of standing there like an idiot.

"No, it's my fault. I was the one who wasn't looking where I was going." She pursed her lips and glanced around. "Did you have a good shower?" Her gaze once again drifted down to my bare chest before snapping back to meet my gaze.

"Yes," I said.

"Good."

An awkward silence fell between us. Juniper had folded her arms across her chest as she glanced around the hallway. I moved to step around her. "I'll get dressed, and then we can head out," I said as I made my way toward the doorway that led to the living room.

"Right. The store." I glanced over my shoulder to see her

nodding as she made her way toward her room. "I'll get ready as well."

Fifteen minutes later, I was dressed and leaning against the counter, sipping a mug of coffee when she walked in. She was wearing a white shirt and a pair of dark denim jeans. Her hair was pulled up into a bun, exposing her long, creamy neck.

The reaction I had to her smile when she saw me startled me into standing up straight. It'd been a long time since a woman looked at me like that, and even though I knew it was innocent, I couldn't help but want it to mean more.

"Everything okay?" she asked as she raised her eyebrows.

I nodded and parted my lips to speak, but nothing came out. I cleared my throat and nodded again. "Yeah...yes," I managed. My body heated with embarrassment.

She studied me, and I could see she wanted to ask me more but didn't know how. The truth was, all I wanted to do was answer her questions, but I knew they involved my past —my mom—and there was no way I was prepared to speak those words out loud.

"It was just a telemarketer." I managed out before I brought my mug to my lips and downed the last of my coffee. Then I walked over to the sink and turned it on. I washed the mug and set it in the drying rack next to the sink.

When I turned, I saw Juniper standing in front of the coffee machine, staring at it. Her eyebrows were drawn together, and her lips were pressed into a line.

"You okay?" I asked as I took a step near her.

She startled and whipped her gaze over to me. She held it there for a moment before she turned back to the machine. "Is coffee bad for babies?"

My body froze. "I...um...I don't know," I admitted.

She wrapped one arm around her stomach and rested the elbow of her other arm on her hand. She brought her hand up to her lips and began chewing on her nail. "I'm just not sure I am going to survive nine months without coffee." Then she paused. "I'm not sure I'm going to survive these nine months in general."

My heart squeezed at how small and fragile she appeared. The instinct washed over me to pull her into my arms and promise to protect her no matter what. Thankfully, I had enough sense to fist my hands and flex my muscles to force myself to remain rooted to my spot.

"Do you have a doctor you can ask?" I finally managed out. Grateful that my head was clear enough to actually process what she was saying.

She glanced over at me. "In Harmony? Ha." She shook her head. "It'll be front page news if I go." She sighed. "The combined curse of living in a small town and being married to the *royalty*." She emphasized the last word with air quotes.

"So you're just not going to go?"

She wrapped both arms around her stomach and turned her attention back to the coffee machine. Silence fell around us as I waited for her to respond. I didn't know a lot about pregnancy and babies, but I knew not involving a doctor could have dire consequences.

Juniper blinked a few times before she turned and smiled at me. "We should go," she said as she dropped her arms and made her way over to the counter to grab her purse. She slipped the strap up onto her shoulder. "We don't want to be late."

I watched her disappear into the living room. Her refusal to answer my question echoed off the walls. I thought about pressing her to find out what her plans were. I wanted her to be safe, and not involving medical professionals in her pregnancy wasn't a safe choice.

But I also knew that pressing her wasn't my place. I had a sinking suspicion that one of the reasons she was so eager to get her parents out of the house was to keep some anonymity. Who was I to take that away from her?

I pushed my hand through my hair as I headed after Juniper. This was her business, not mine. If she needed to take her time before going to see a doctor, who was I to say otherwise? I wasn't her family. And I certainly wasn't her husband or the father of her baby.

I was...nobody.

And I was pretty sure that was who I would remain.

6

ELLA

SWEET TEA & SOUTHERN GENTLEMAN

"Ella, can you come in here, please?"

Gloria's voice snapped me to attention. I hadn't noticed that I was leaning into my computer while editing my latest piece about the updates that Mayor Jorgenson wanted to make to the Harmony Island bridge that connected us to the mainland. I had been so lost in the words that my posture had taken a hit.

"Yes, Gloria," I called as I pushed out my chair and stood. I smoothed down my pencil skirt and picked up the notebook and pen that I kept on my desk for these impromptu meetings.

Gloria was sitting in front of her computer with her glasses perched on her nose. She was staring at the screen as her hand moved the mouse around. I stood in the doorway, waiting for her invitation to enter. After a few seconds, she settled back into her chair and motioned for me to sit on one of the chairs in front of her. I nodded and obeyed, my pen poised over the notebook so I was ready for whatever she needed me to do.

She bounced a few times in her chair before she rested her elbows on the armrests and steepled her fingers. "I need you to take Elizabeth with you to Harmony Cove."

I jotted down *Harmony Cove* in my notebook. It was one of the oldest parts of town. The houses were small and dated but had the best view of the island. Most of the Harmony Island originals lived there. "Okay, I can do that." Then I glanced up at her. "Any particular reason why?"

Gloria studied me as if she was weighing her words. Then she sighed and sat up. She started straightening things on her desk as she spoke. "Marcus Proctor has requested that we run a cover piece on the offers they are making to the residents of Harmony Cove. They are on their way right now to extend the offer to Barbara McDonnell and would like newspaper coverage."

My pen hovered over the notebook as I processed what she was saying. As much as I'd wanted to put the mystery man from the day before behind me, hearing the Proctor name made that resolution fly from my mind.

It took me a moment to realize that Gloria had stopped talking, so I quickly jotted down what she'd said. "Sounds easy enough," I said with a smile. I raised my eyebrows. "Anything else?"

Gloria was studying me. I could tell that she wanted to say more, but I was determined to get her off the scent. If she wasn't going to sanction me looking into the Proctor family, then I was just going to have to do some digging on my own. Maybe it was nothing. Maybe Gloria and Asher were right.

But maybe—and this was less likely—maybe they were wrong.

It's a journalist's responsibility to ask questions and seek for truth even if it made people uncomfortable.

"No," Gloria said as she narrowed her eyes. "Just that story and nothing else." Then she paused. "I'll text you the address."

I set my pen down on my notebook, hooking it with my thumb to keep it in place, and moved to stand. "Wonderful. I'll go grab Elizabeth, and we'll head out."

I could feel Gloria's stare on me as I gave her a quick nod and headed out of her office. Elizabeth was sitting behind her desk, typing away on her keyboard when I walked up to her. I tapped her desk a few times to get her attention. Elizabeth was the intern Gloria had hired. She had just graduated from Harmony High last year, and she did a lot of the grunt work. She was young but sweet and willing to do whatever she needed to do for Gloria. I enjoyed her company when I was asked to bring her with me.

"We've got a story to cover," I said when she finally stopped typing and looked up at me through her glasses with multi-colored rims.

Her ears perked as she nodded. "You've got it, boss."

I gave her a quick smile before heading over to my desk.

I grabbed my purse, my voice recorder, a notebook, and pens. After sliding the items into my bag, I fished out my keys, grabbed my half empty coffee cup, and pushed in my chair.

I was filling my cup with coffee when Elizabeth walked up to me. She had on a cute brimmed hat and was pulling her purse strap up onto her shoulder.

"Ready?" I asked as she pulled out a pair of sunglasses from her purse and swapped her glasses for them.

"Yep," she said as she settled the sunglasses onto her nose.

"Great." I replaced the coffee pot and screwed on the lid to my cup. My keys jangled in my hand as I grabbed the now full coffee cup while using my other hand to find my sunglasses that I was sure were buried in the bottom of my purse.

The sun was bright when I pushed the front door open. I slipped my glasses on as I held the door for Elizabeth, and we headed toward my car.

I gave Elizabeth a sheepish smile as I hurried to clear the takeout boxes scattered in my front seat. I never really drove anyone else. If Asher and I hung out, we normally just drove separately. Besides a few acquaintances here on the island, I didn't have any bosom buddies. I was hoping ladies like Abigail and Shelby were going to fix that.

Once we were settled, I stuck the key into the ignition, and my car roared to life. It was only a fifteen-minute drive to Harmony Cove. Jack Johnson played on my radio as I turned into the community.

The sign that greeted us was weatherworn but beautiful. The wood sign was intricately carved with images of flowers and the sun. The letters of *Harmony Cove* curved and swirled. Its white paint was in need of a refresh, but even in its aged state, it was a work of art.

"What's happening in Harmony Cove?" Elizabeth asked as she shifted her gaze from outside the window to me.

"Proctors wanted us here to cover some offer they are making to Barbara McDonnell," I said as I fished around my cupholder for my phone. Once in hand, I held it out in front of me while I shifted my gaze from my phone to the road. Thankfully, it only took me a moment to find Gloria's text, and I read the address out loud to Elizabeth.

After two right turns, we pulled up behind a row of black SUVs. My tiny Toyota Corolla looked minuscule next to them. I looked over at Elizabeth, who looked just as confused as I was. Why were there so many vehicles here if they were just making an offer on Ms. McDonnell's house?

We both unbuckled at the same time. I grabbed my purse and hiked it up onto my shoulder as I pushed open the driver's door and climbed out. Elizabeth waited for me as I rounded the hood. We walked side by side down the sidewalk and up Ms. McDonnell's driveway.

A man in a dark suit and sunglasses stood next to the front door. This seemed a little excessive for what we'd been asked to come down here and cover. I shot Elizabeth a look and she responded by raising her eyebrows.

"Excuse me," the bouncer-looking man said as he stepped forward and held up his hand. "What can I help you with?"

"I'm Ella Calipso." I shoved my hand into my purse. Gloria had given me a press badge when I started, but this was such a small town I'd never had to take it out. People just knew who I was, and if they didn't, they certainly knew Gloria. "With Harmony Gazette," I added when no recognition passed over the man's face.

He narrowed his eyes before he stepped back and lifted his wrist to his mouth and muttered something. Whomever he'd talked to must have given Elizabeth and me the green light because he suddenly walked over to the door and pulled it open. With a flick of his hand, he motioned for us to enter.

"Thanks," I said as I led Elizabeth up the porch steps and through the front door. The entire exchange was so weird. Why were they acting like the president was here? I wanted to turn and ask Elizabeth what she thought, but I also wanted to appear professional, and two whispering, gossiping girls walking into a meeting didn't seem to be the way to portray that.

I could hear voices coming from the back of the house, so I headed down the hallway with Elizabeth right behind me. Everyone was in the kitchen. Marcus Proctor was sitting at the head of the table with Ms. McDonnell next to him.

There was a group of men in suits standing behind Marcus, and standing to the left was...

I frowned. Asher?

His gaze caught mine, and he looked as confused as I did as he stared at me. I could see the question forming in his mind, and it matched my own, *what are you doing here?*

"Ah, you must be who Gloria sent," Mr. Proctor said as he waved me over.

Not sure what to do, I obeyed and walked closer to him. "Ella," I said when I got close enough to extend my hand. "Ella Calipso."

Mr. Proctor glanced down at my hand, and for a moment, I worried that I'd overstepped. Thankfully, he took my hand and shook it before nodding toward the empty seat at the other end of the table.

Not wanting to draw even more attention to myself, I hurried to the spot and took a seat. Elizabeth sat to my left. I pulled out my notebook, pen, and recorder and set them on the table. It seemed as if everyone was waiting for me to finish before they started talking. I pressed record and then uncapped my pen and held the tip over my notebook.

"As I was saying," Mr. Proctor said, "we think that an offer of $1.3 million is very generous." His gaze focused on Ms. McDonnell, who was studying the tabletop in front of her.

I almost choked when I heard that amount leave his lips. My gaze instantly snapped over to Asher, who glanced at me. I raised my eyebrows, but he just kept his expression stoic as he slightly shook his head and focused back on Ms. McDonnell.

"It's life changing money," Mr. Proctor continued.

Ms. McDonnell nodded. "I know," she whispered. "I guess I just never thought about selling. This is where I've lived my whole life. Teddy and I brought our babies home here." Ms. McDonnell reached her wrinkled hand out and rested it on the table. My heart ached for her. She reminded me of my grandmother.

Mr. Proctor glanced around the room as if he were looking for someone to back him up. His gaze settled on Asher. My friend paused but then nodded as if he understood exactly what Mr. Proctor wanted from him.

"Listen, Barbara. This is an amazing deal. I would suggest you take it. The housing market can be a volatile one, and in the regular market, you won't get near this much." He leaned forward, his lips tipped up into a smile. "The Proctors are offering top dollar because they are making an investment. If you sell on the open market, a regular buyer won't be able to pay as much."

Ms. McDonnell was studying him as he spoke. I could see her expression soften as Asher spoke. $1.3 million was quite a lot. If Asher thought it was a good deal, she should trust him even if I didn't trust Mr. Proctor.

I watched with my pen poised above my notepad to continue writing. It was as if the whole room was holding their collective breath to see what she was going to say. Ms.

McDonnell dropped her gaze to the table and paused before she slowly started to nod.

"Okay," she whispered. "I'll sell."

The entire room erupted into celebration as the suits standing behind Mr. Proctor began talking. Briefcases were opened and papers were shuffled as the men surrounded Ms. McDonnell. I kept my gaze on Mr. Proctor, whose smile gave me an uneasy feeling in my stomach. He was speaking to a man next to him before he turned to Asher and spoke in a hushed tone.

I wished I could get closer to hear what he was saying, but that would look weird and, after my conversation with Asher last night, I didn't want him to think I wasn't being a supportive friend. If he was going to get a piece of the $1.3 million pie, I didn't want to be the negative Nelly standing in the way of his celebration.

"I think that's it," I said as I gathered my items and shoved them back into my purse. I wasn't sure exactly what I was going to write a whole article about, and I had a sinking suspicion that Gloria was going to help me write it with a heavy hand.

I grabbed my phone from my purse as I stood. I needed to grab a few photos for the article before I left. I waved for Elizabeth to wait as I rounded the table and moved my phone around for a good shot of Ms. McDonnell signing the papers that were being laid in front of her one by one.

She looked overwhelmed as she scribbled her signature on each form. After a few shots, I stuffed my phone back into my purse and turned. I yelped when I saw Asher standing next to me with the widest smile I'd ever seen. He wiggled his eyebrows before he quickly glanced around to make sure no one saw what he'd just done.

"Are you working tonight?" he asked as I stepped around him. He followed a few inches behind me so only I could hear his voice.

"Probably," I said as I nodded to Elizabeth as I walked by her. She understood my gesture and followed behind Asher.

"Well, can you get out of it?" he asked as we left the dining room and entered the hallway.

"Asher, where are you going?" Mr. Proctor's voice boomed over the other conversations.

"Be right back, Marcus." Asher popped back into the middle of the doorway and nodded toward Mr. Proctor, who seemed okay with his response and returned to talking to the balding man next to him.

I couldn't shake the feeling in my stomach that something was off. And as much as I wanted to hang out with my friend, I knew he wanted to talk about this deal and he was going to want me to share in his excitement.

I just wasn't ready for that.

"I'll have to see what Gloria wants. She's in a mood today, and I doubt she'll want me to bail on her." I forced a smile. "I'll text you, though."

He was staring down at me. His gaze was conflicted. I knew he wanted a solid answer—and for that answer to be yes—but I wasn't ready to give it to him. I needed some time to process, and I couldn't do that with his smiling face in front of mine all evening.

"Yeah, okay. I get it." He turned to Elizabeth. "Make sure she at least *tries* to take the evening off," he said as he pointed his finger directly at her.

Elizabeth gave him a mock salute. That seemed to appease Asher as he turned back to me and narrowed his eyes for a moment before he pulled me into a hug. "I'm glad you're in Harmony." He held me for a moment and then broke away.

"Me too," I whispered, but he was already heading back into the dining room by the time I got the words out.

It took me a moment to get my bearings and turn to Elizabeth. She was scrolling on her phone, so I bumped her shoulder with mine and said, "Let's go." She tucked her phone into her back pocket and nodded. She followed me out of the house and over to my car.

We drove in silence. When we were a few minutes from the newspaper, she spoke. "I can cover for you if you want," she said, glancing over at me and giving me a shy smile. "I don't know what the story is between you and that guy, but he really seems to like you."

I scoffed. "Asher?"

She nodded.

"Asher's just my friend." I shook my head as I paused before taking a left turn. "He's always just been my friend."

I glanced over at Elizabeth when she didn't respond. I

had this desire to keep going, but I knew from experience overexplaining always raised suspicions.

It wasn't until I'd parked behind the newspaper that Elizabeth decided to respond. She opened the door and turned to smile at me. "If you say so," she said before she climbed out and shut the door behind her.

I was left sputtering, attempting to refute her words, but it was too late. I watched her walk away from my car, across the parking lot, and disappear into the building, the door swinging shut behind her.

7

JUNIPER

SWEET TEA & SOUTHERN GENTLEMAN

The morning went smoother than I'd anticipated. Boone was uncomplicated and focused, which helped me relax as we went through the daily motions of opening the store. Without Mom and Dad here complicating things, we were able to finish the prep work and chat with Sal and Katie when they walked in.

I set up shop at the register, while Boone chose to walk the aisles and stock the shelves. If I needed assistance, all I needed to do was call him over the intercom and he'd come open a register.

By lunchtime, the store was humming with life and the sound of the register scanning each item. I was in a rhythm, and for the first time in a long time, I felt...relaxed.

And I was enjoying it.

Mrs. Dodd handed me a twenty after I rang up her bananas, three yogurts, a half gallon of milk, and a chocolate bar. I took the money from her, typed the amount into the computer, and my register drawer opened so I could get her change.

"Where's your mother?" she asked as I handed her the money.

"With my dad. They're headed to California to help my aunt—Mom's sister."

Mrs. Dodd's eyes widened. "I hope everything's okay."

I knew how private my mom was. The last thing she'd want me to do was share my aunt's business all over town. So I just forced a smile and said, "It's just a visit. They'll be back in a few days."

Mrs. Dodd nodded as she tucked the money into its respective spots. "She's lucky to have such a loyal daughter like you," she said as she raised her gaze to meet mine. "I know she's been missing you since you left. It's good that you came back."

Guilt, shame, and anger flooded my body at her words. Guilt that I let Kevin keep me away for so long. Shame that I hadn't been stronger and stood up for myself. Anger that I was still keeping things from my parents even though they'd so willingly taken me back.

I was a terrible daughter.

I forced a smile and handed Mrs. Dodd her receipt. She took it and bid me farewell as she turned and headed toward the automatic doors. I collapsed against the register and took in a few deep breaths. Who was I kidding? Why did I think

I could actually feel peace when my life was in shambles. And it was all my fault.

"When do you want to go to lunch?" Boone's voice drew me from the fog in my head. I turned to see him standing behind me. My feelings must have been written on my face because his expression turned serious as he took a step toward me. "What's wrong? Is he here?" His body stiffened as he glanced around the store.

I raised my hand and shook my head. "No. I'm okay," I lied as I straightened and smoothed down my shirt. "Just a bout of nausea." I cleared my throat. "Lunch?"

He glanced down at me before glancing around the store one more time. I could tell by his expression that he wasn't fully convinced, but I'd learned enough about Boone by now to know that he wasn't going to push me—unlike my mother. If I said nothing was wrong, he would accept it, even if he was skeptical.

"Yeah," he said as he pushed his hand through his hair. "If you want to go, I can watch the register."

My stomach grumbled in response. I was ready to eat. "Um, sure." I turned back to the register and then back to him. "Yeah, I can go."

His gaze met mine. "Only if you want to."

My lips tipped up into a soft smile. Boone was...different. Kevin always told me where to go and when. He never asked me what I wanted. I was his wife. His property. I didn't have a say even when it came to what I wanted.

Hearing Boone make sure I was okay with taking a break was nice.

I liked making my own decisions.

"I do. I'm hungry, and if I don't eat I'll get nauseous."

Boone's gaze drifted down to my stomach before he nodded. "Okay."

"Thanks." I patted his arm as I passed. He stiffened, and for a moment I wondered if I'd overstepped. But then I pushed those thoughts from my mind. Boone and I were friends. He knew more about me than anyone else in my life.

I walked to the meat counter to pick up one of Sal's famous sandwiches. After grabbing a bag of Funyuns, I slid back the door to the drink cooler and grabbed a Sprite before I made my way to the register to pay.

There were two people in front of me when I got in line. Boone was quiet as he scanned each item. The woman who was standing there, watching her groceries, was about my age. I'd never seen her before, but that didn't mean anything. There were a lot of new people in town.

She was desperately trying to engage Boone in conversation. Her smile was wide, and her laugh was loud whenever she was able to get a few words from him. Their connection would only last for a moment before Boone dropped his gaze to focus on scanning the food. I could tell that Boone felt uncomfortable, but the woman didn't seem to realize she was bothering him.

She kept talking, and at one point, she reached over and

touched his hand. Anger rose up inside of me as I watched the interaction. I didn't like that this woman thought she could just come in here and touch the employees. I also didn't like that she couldn't pick up on the fact that he was uncomfortable. Sure, Boone was hot. He had this brooding, mysterious element to him that would pique any woman's interest, but he was so much more than that. And for some strange reason, it was frustrating me that she couldn't see that.

Thankfully, the woman ran out of groceries to scan. She glanced around as if she were looking for something else to pick up, but Boone motioned toward the credit card machine and told her the total. The woman pulled her card from her purse while asking him if he was free Friday night. I held my breath, waiting to hear what he was going to say.

Sure, he was helping me with the store Friday during the day, but he had no obligation to hang out with me Friday night. I didn't like the idea of him going out with this stranger who seemed a little too eager to get to know him... but I also knew that I had no right to ask him to stay with me.

"I'm busy," Boone said as the register spit out her receipt. He tore it from the machine and handed it over to the woman.

She took it and then paused before she reached over the register and grabbed a pen. She held it poised over the paper as she glanced up at Boone. "Can I give you my number in case you change your mind?" she asked as she flashed him a big smile.

Boone must have said something to reject her because her expression fell as he spoke to her. She forced a smile before she wrapped her hands around her shopping cart, and pushed it toward the sliding doors. She gave him one last longing look before she disappeared out to the parking lot.

The guy in front of me had an energy drink and a doughnut, which Boone scanned quickly. He ran his card, took his bag, and hurried from the store.

Boone looked over at me, and his expression softened as the conveyor belt activated, pulling my items toward him.

I stood there, studying him as he rang up my items. I couldn't shake his interaction with that woman from my mind. Why hadn't he said yes? The woman was clearly interested and was determined to make things *very* easy for him. Most guys would have flirted back if only for the confidence boost.

Why didn't Boone seem remotely interested? What was his story?

"Everything okay?" Boone's voice ripped through my reverie.

I startled, standing straight and clearing my throat. "Yea—yes. Yes. Everything is fine." I tucked my hair behind my ear and brought my gaze up to meet his.

He was studying me with an amused smile on his lips.

"What?" I asked as I moved my attention to the card machine, waiting for the total to appear.

"Nothing." There was something in his tone and the smooth way that word left his lips that frustrated me. It was like he was reading me when it was almost impossible to read him. It really wasn't fair.

"You don't smile at me like that when it's nothing," I blurted out as I slipped my card into the reader just as the total came up on the screen. When Boone didn't answer, I glanced back up at him.

His eyebrows were drawn together. "How do I smile at you?" he asked. The register came to life as it spit out the receipt. He didn't pull his gaze from mine as he reached over and tore it off. He held it in his hand as he studied me.

There was a depth to his gaze as he lingered. Zaps of electricity sparked around us, and for a moment, it felt like the world had slowed.

Then suddenly, Boone dropped his gaze, shoved the receipt toward me, and mumbled something about enjoying my lunch break. Before I could respond, he pulled out his phone, leaned against the counter, and started scrolling.

I paused, wondering if I'd done something wrong. But then I shook my head and grabbed the grocery bag that held my lunch. Boone was a strange one. There were moments he let down that guard he'd formed around himself. There were moments when I got to see the real Boone. But then, as soon as he realized what he'd done, he'd go right back to the aloof, standoffish guy I met the first day he showed up at the store.

I made my way to the back break room, my mind swirling with questions but knowing that I really didn't have the right to ask any of them. The best thing I could do for myself was to just let them go. Boone was here for a short period of time. As soon as Kevin left Harmony, Boone would no longer be needed.

I couldn't imagine Kevin staying much longer if he hadn't left already. Every time we returned to Harmony, the longest he could stand was a few days before we were packing up our suitcases and heading back to Texas. I was hopeful that he would keep the habit this go-around.

I set my lunch down on the table and pulled out a chair. After I'd opened the bag of chips and drink, I propped my phone against the napkin dispenser on the table and unwrapped the sandwich as I watched reels on my phone.

My sandwich was half gone when I heard a noise behind me. I grabbed a napkin from the dispenser and wiped my mouth as I turned to see what it was. My entire body froze when I saw Kevin standing in the doorway, sweeping his gaze around the room. When it settled on me, all I wanted to do was throw up and run away.

"Hey, sweetheart," he said as he stepped into the room.

My body stiffened as he walked closer to me. I wanted to tell him to leave me alone. I wanted the strength to get up and run away. But I was rooted to my chair, and I couldn't form coherent sentences much less strategize how to get out of this situation.

The sound of chair legs scraping across the cement floor echoed against the walls. He plopped down on the chair next to mine and extended his legs out, one underneath my chair and the other behind the back chair legs, effectively trapping me.

He reached forward and grabbed the bag of chips and began eating them. He had a few before he wrinkled his nose and dropped the bag back down on the table. "Bleh. I will never understand why you like those," he said, flicking the bag across the table with the back of his hand. "They're nasty."

My mouth was dry. It was taking all my strength not to hurl up my lunch. It was a strange feeling, not being able to get enough moisture in my mouth but my glands tingling as my stomach churned.

Kevin leaned forward until his face was inches from mine. His hand found my leg, and he began to slowly drag his palm and fingertips up my thigh. "I miss you, baby," he whispered. "When are you going to come back home?" He tucked his hand between my legs and held it there.

I wanted to scream. I wanted to run. But my body wasn't responding to anything. He had this hold on me. I hated how weak and helpless I felt when he touched me. All I wanted was the strength to protect myself, but it never came. Instead I just froze, taking whatever punishment he wanted to dish out.

"I heard your parents are out of town." He leaned forward and pressed his lips to my temple. "I can come over if you want. You can't tell me that you don't miss me, too."

I closed my eyes, hating that there was a part of me that still wanted to say yes. Kevin had been my world for so long. I didn't know who I was without him. But my situation had changed since I walked away from him. I was pregnant with his baby, even though he didn't know that.

I wasn't sure how I was going to tell him, but I knew the break room of Godwin's Grocery wasn't the place.

"Let's get some dinner, first," I finally managed out as I turned to face him.

He raised his eyebrows but didn't pull back. "Dinner?"

I nodded. "Tonight."

He smiled. "Sounds amazing." His phone buzzed, forcing him to sit up straight. He pulled his phone from his back pocket and glanced at the screen before he tucked the phone away. "Gotta go, babe," he said as he leaned forward and gave me a quick peck on the lips. It happened so fast that I didn't have time to pull away. The last thing I wanted was to kiss him. "I'll send you a text with the address and time of the reservation." He shoved his chair back as he stood. "Dress nice."

I nodded but kept my focus on the table in front of me. Kevin mumbled a quick goodbye and didn't wait for my reply. He was gone before I looked up.

Now alone, I let out the breath that I'd been holding. I reached forward to grab my sandwich. My hands were shaking as I wrapped it back up. My stomach was too volatile to put anything else in it.

I kept glancing toward the doorway, waiting for Kevin to come back. It took five full minutes for my body to start to relax. With each ticking minute, Kevin was getting further and further away from the store, which meant I was safe. He wasn't going to just appear again.

With my lunch packaged in the plastic bag I'd gotten from Boone, I leaned back in my seat, crossing my arms over my chest in an effort to feel more in control of myself. I closed my eyes and took in a few deep breaths.

This was not how I saw today going.

I'd secretly wished that Kevin had left Harmony, but he hadn't. I'd secretly wished that Kevin would let me go, but he wouldn't. And I'd stupidly deluded myself into thinking that our relationship was over, when it wasn't.

Kevin hadn't let me go even after I'd made it clear that I wasn't interested in being together. He was going to have the final say. I would always be his. Which meant the baby was his as well. Even though he'd never wanted a child, he'd use it to control me.

I pressed my hand to my stomach, loving the baby growing there but hating the situation it was being born into.

I wanted to believe I could be strong, but after this inter-action with Kevin, my confidence was crumbling. And the last thing I wanted to gamble with was our child's safety.

I was determined to find the strength inside of me to walk away, and when I did, it needed to be for good.

8

BOONE

SWEET TEA & SOUTHERN GENTLEMAN

Juniper came back from lunch looking paler than when she'd left. I wanted to ask her if everything was okay, but she didn't look like she was interested in talking and I didn't want to overstep. I knew one of the reasons she pushed her parents out this morning was so she could have some privacy. I wasn't about to pry and lose the small amount of trust she seemed willing to give me.

So when she appeared next to me to take over the register, I gave her a quick smile, gathered my things, and stepped out of the way.

I grabbed a sandwich from Sal and a soda. After Juniper rang me up, I ate quickly in the break room. I had a few more voicemails from Collin Baker, but I just deleted them without listening. I wasn't ready to face my mother's house just yet, and no pushy acquisitions guy was going to force me to.

Once my food was gone, I didn't wait to finish my break. I grabbed my garbage and tossed it into the trash on my way out. The store was quiet when I pushed through the swinging doors.

I could see Juniper by the register. She was leaning against the counter, looking down at her phone. I glanced around to see if her mother's chair was there, but I didn't see it. So I spent the next five minutes hunting it down.

Juniper glanced up as I neared. Her gaze drifted from my face down to the chair I was carrying. Her expression was stoic as she left the register alcove so I could enter.

My heart sunk as I set the chair down. I don't know why I thought she would break into a big smile. She just seemed so down, and all I wanted was to see her smile. It was gnawing at me that she was this unhappy.

"Thought you might need this," I said, feeling stupid that I wanted to be her hero. I was bringing her a chair to sit on, not solving all of her life's issues.

"Thanks," she whispered.

I set the chair down and turned to face her. Her lips were more relaxed now, and the worry lines that had creased her forehead earlier were gone. I was going to take that as a win even though I wanted so much more.

"I'm going to finish stocking the cheese," I announced as I straightened and stepped out of the alcove so she could step inside.

Juniper glanced toward the cheese refrigerator along the back wall. "Okay."

I paused, wanting to ask her if everything was okay, but I forced those words down my throat and pushed my hand through my hair. "Call me on the intercom if you need anything."

She nodded and settled down onto the chair. She didn't look at me. Instead, she picked up her phone and returned to scrolling.

I spent the next few hours cursing myself for being so stupid. How had I allowed myself to become so enamored with a woman I'd only just met? Every time I tried to push her from my mind, her soft, creamy skin and full pink lips invaded my thoughts. She seemed so small and fragile that all I wanted to do was protect her—even though I was constantly telling myself she wasn't mine to protect.

The evening sun was shining into the store when I wheeled the stock cart to the back room and emerged back into the store. I cracked my neck and fingers as I glanced around, wondering what I should do next.

I made my way to the front of the store, where I saw Juniper talking to a girl with blonde hair. She was smiling as Juniper talked. Juniper looked so at ease, and then they both broke out into a laugh. It was the sound of Juniper's laughter that caused me to quicken my pace as I made my way toward them. It was so full of life. I'd felt dead for so long my body warmed from the sound, and I instantly needed more.

"Hey, Boone," Juniper said when her gaze fell on me. I hadn't expected her to acknowledge me, and I certainly didn't expect the way my heart picked up speed as she turned her smile on me. "Have you met Shelby yet?"

The blonde woman turned to me and offered me a smile. "It's nice to meet you, Boone," she said as she extended her hand.

"Shelby married Miles. They run The Harmony Island Inn."

I remembered the inn, but neither name was familiar to me. So I just shook Shelby's hand and said, "It's nice to meet you."

"My parents hired Boone to help out around here," Juniper said. "It's been nice to have someone help me run this place while they're gone."

Shelby glanced over at Juniper before she settled her gaze on me. "You're awesome for doing that."

I didn't like praise. As soon as the words hit my ears, a black cloud moved through my body. Not wanting to stand there under their approving gazes, I shoved my hands into my front pockets and turned my attention to Juniper.

"I was thinking about grabbing some steaks for dinner tonight." I paused, wondering if it was too presumptuous for me to think she would actually want to eat with me. "Er...I mean if you wanted me to make you something."

Juniper's cheeks flushed, and I wasn't sure what to make of that. She dropped gaze for a moment before she brought it up to meet mine. "I actually have dinner plans," she said, her voice low and hushed.

I glanced over at Shelby, who was shifting her gaze

between me and Juniper. Realization dawned on me. She was probably eating out with Shelby. This felt awkward.

"Oh, okay," I said quickly. Ready to get far away from this embarrassing situation, I gave them a quick nod before I turned and headed toward the back room.

Once I was through the swinging doors, I moved to the nearby corner and took in a few deep breaths. I closed my eyes and forced my feelings to the dark corners of my mind. I hated that I felt so drawn to Juniper. I was sad that she wasn't going to be eating dinner with me and I wanted to know what she was doing. But she didn't have any obligation to tell me, and it wasn't my place to ask.

I was the biggest idiot.

Not wanting Juniper to find me back here slowly losing my mind, I rolled my shoulders and stilled my thoughts. Juniper wasn't mine to worry about and I needed to stop acting like she was. I was going to head back out there and grab food to make myself some dinner. Then I was going to drive home, eat, and go to bed.

And I was going to do all of that while *not* thinking about Juniper.

Juniper was talking to Jordan, who was filling in as evening cashier and store closer, when I finally put myself together and walked out from the back room. Juniper was running over what Jordan needed to do to close up the store as she rang up the items I'd picked up for dinner. Jordan nodded after every few words. Tim would be here in a few minutes to help. With Mr. and Mrs. Godwin gone, they were calling in reinforcements, and since I was so new, I hadn't met them yet. Which was okay. I really didn't have a plan to make Harmony my final stop.

The fewer people I got to know the better.

I kept to the back, waiting for Juniper to finish. We'd driven to the store together, so I couldn't leave without her. The grocery bag handles dug into my fingers as it hung near my leg. I shifted my weight as Juniper nodded along to whatever Jordan was saying.

Suddenly, Juniper's gaze drifted over to me, and I realized that I was staring at her. I cleared my throat and dropped my gaze to the ground. What was I thinking? Why had I been watching her that hard?

What was wrong with me?

I heard Juniper's steps before I saw her shoes appear in front of me. She cleared her throat, so I brought my gaze up to meet hers.

"Sorry that took so long," she said, a soft smile playing on her lips. "I wanted to make sure that Jordan knew what needed to be done."

"I understand," I said quickly. "I was fine waiting." I didn't want her to think that the reason I'd been staring at her was because I wanted her to hurry along. I'd been happy to stand there watching her all evening. I gave her a quick smile, and she just studied me before she nodded.

"Let's go."

She headed through the swinging doors to the back room and walked into her mom's office to grab her things. I waited in the hallway, leaning against the wall with my legs extended. I forced my mind to still, too scared of where my thoughts might go if I let them wander too far.

She appeared in the doorway a few minutes later. My gaze snapped right to her, and I watched as she flipped off the light, closed the office door, and locked it before dropping her keychain into her purse.

"Ready?" she asked as she met my gaze.

I nodded.

She led the way through the hall to the back door. When she paused at the door, I leaned forward to push it open for her. Her startled gaze met mine.

"Thanks," she whispered.

"Of course." I waited for her to pass through before I followed.

The outer door slammed behind me. I unlocked my truck with the key fob and hurried to the passenger door to open it for her. Once again, her gaze snapped to me. Her eyes were wide. "Thanks," she said.

I just nodded this time while I waited for her to get into the truck. Once she was in and situated, I shut the door and jogged around the hood of the truck. My chest brushed her shoulder as I twisted to put my bag of groceries in the back seat.

I prayed she couldn't hear my pounding heart as I turned to face the steering wheel. In an effort to distract myself, I shoved my car key into the ignition and turned the engine on. I threw my truck into reverse and pulled out of the parking spot.

We were headed down Main Street when I felt Juniper's gaze on me. I wanted to turn to look at her but decided against it. Instead, I just kept my focus on the road. When I got to the stoplight, I took a second to pull my phone from my back pocket and set it into the cupholder. It had been jabbing me.

"Fun plans for tonight?" I asked as I squeezed the steering wheel and waited for the light to turn green. When she didn't respond, I turned to see if she'd heard me. Her cheeks were pink and she was staring at her hands in her lap. Her lips were pulled together in a line. I leaned forward to catch her gaze so I could give her a comforting smile. "Everything okay?" I asked for what felt like the millionth time today.

She sighed and glanced out the window before turning her attention to me. "I just have that dinner I have to go to." Her smile was small and there was an intense pain in her gaze. "So I wouldn't say *fun*." She grew quiet for a moment as her gaze drifted outside. "It's just necessary."

"Oh." The light turned green so I pressed on the gas. She wasn't saying much, and it made me wonder if it was because she was seeing Kevin. Was he still in town? "Aren't you going out with Shelby?"

Juniper glanced over at me before she folded her arms across chest. "Listen, Boone, I'm grateful for your help at the store and everything. But I think it's okay if we don't know everything about each other." She smiled at me. "You live your life, and I'll live mine."

Her words hit me like a ton of bricks and made me feel like an idiot. Of course she felt that way. I'd stepped into her territory, and I didn't belong. Maybe I'd deluded myself into thinking that we were friends. It was clear that she wasn't interested in even being that.

"Gotcha," I said as I stared hard at the road in front of me. "I won't pry."

I could tell from the few times she glanced over at me that she wanted to say something. I wondered if she felt like she'd been too harsh but didn't know what to say to fix it. Truth was, I'd needed her words like a glass of ice-cold water dumped over my head. They had been the wake-up call I needed. I'd overstepped, and she had every right to slap my hand.

I was grateful that she did.

I pulled into the Godwins' driveway and turned off the engine. Juniper lingered in her seat, so I stayed put as well in case she had something she wanted to say to me. We sat in silence until the loud, shrill sound of my phone ringing pierced the air. Both of our gazes snapped to the screen.

Collin Baker flashed under the phone number. I shook my head as I reached out to hang up. I wasn't going to talk to him now or ever. I kept my phone in my hand as I opened the driver's door and climbed out.

Juniper beat me to opening her door, so I focused on grabbing my dinner fixings from the back seat. By the time I turned toward the house, she'd disappeared inside. I took a moment to stare at the door. For a moment, I allowed myself to wonder if she was standing on the other side before I shook my head and crossed the space between my car and the house.

Of course, she wasn't standing there. Only an idiot would think that. And once again, I was proving to myself how much of an idiot I was. Juniper wasn't my friend. She certainly wasn't my girlfriend. I was nothing to her, and I would do well to remember that. Now and in the future.

I came to Harmony to settle Mom's estate and bury the past. It was time I started working on that.

9

JUNIPER

SWEET TEA & SOUTHERN GENTLEMAN

I felt bad as I walked away from Boone. He really was the nicest guy, and I didn't know what to do with that. I just knew that I wanted to keep Boone as far away from Kevin as possible. The last thing I wanted was for him to get entrenched in my messy marriage. The less he knew the better.

It was healthier for everyone to keep Boone on the outskirts of my life rather than draw him in. I'd already entangled him in my mess. The least I could do was keep him from being drawn further into the natural disaster that was my marriage.

I leaned against the door after I'd shut it. The image of Boone standing by his car holding a grocery bag in one hand with his dark gaze focused on me felt forever burned into my retinas. I felt guilty for leaving him in the dark. The truth was, I *wanted* to tell him. I liked him knowing things about me. Talking to him felt as easy as breathing.

But I wanted to keep him safe, and with Kevin still in Harmony, Boone was anything but safe. Distance was good. Distance was necessary.

My phone chimed, causing my watch to vibrate. I glanced down to see that Kevin had texted me. It was an address and time. Seven o'clock. It was currently six. I still needed to shower and get dressed.

I pushed off the door and headed through the kitchen to my room. I slipped out of my Godwin's Grocery shirt and khakis. I took a fast shower and towel dried. I used my hand to wipe the steam from the mirror and stared at my reflection.

Kevin's handiwork had disappeared. I reached up and gingerly touched my cheekbone. The bruise was gone, so was the pain that followed any pressure to the site. But the pain of what he did to me remained. My body no longer held the physical manifestation of his abuse, but my soul would forever be scarred. And I was never going to heal from the pain he inflicted on me.

I shook my head as I opened the top drawer to my vanity and pulled out my foundation. I wasn't taking Kevin back. I'd already made up my mind. We were finished. I was going to pay a visit to the lawyer to get the paperwork started. I was no longer his wife, and he was no longer my husband.

I just needed to suss out how he felt about the baby

without actually saying he was going to be a dad. If he repeated what he'd said from the beginning of our marriage—that a baby was not in his future—then I would walk away without telling him. I needed to do what was right for the baby, and being some trophy for Kevin to parade around would kill that child.

I wasn't willing to hurt someone so innocent.

Tears pricked my eyes as I pressed my hand into my stomach. I wished I could change the situation this baby was going to be born into. I would give anything to give them the family and future they deserved. I felt so selfish to for trying to allow myself to be happy. How could I be happy bringing a child into this mess?

I closed my eyes and stifled a sob that was trying to escape my lips. I shook my head, feeling so frustrated with myself for being so weak. This baby needed a strong mom. Not someone so weak she couldn't get herself together enough to do her makeup and go to dinner.

I blew out my breath. Once all the air had left my lungs, I opened my eyes and stared at my reflection in the mirror. I was going to be strong. I *needed* to be strong.

I had no more room for weakness. This baby was counting on me.

I finished my makeup, pulled off my microfiber head wrap, and combed my fingers through my damp hair. I would diffuse it once I was dressed and my curls had some time to dry on their own.

I settled on a calf-length floral dress. It had puffy sleeves and made me feel feminine yet strong. I walked back into the bathroom and turned on my hair dryer. After my hair fell in soft curls around my face, I inspected my reflection one last time before switching off my bathroom light and gathering my white sandals and purse.

I pulled open my bedroom door and glanced down the hallway, wondering where Boone was. The sound of someone cooking carried from the kitchen, so I turned that direction. After all, I was going to have to go through the kitchen to get out to my car. I might as well get my interaction with Boone over with.

I paused when I got to the doorway that led into the kitchen. Boone was standing at the sink, washing a pan. His back was to me, so I took a moment to study him. He was wearing a white t-shirt and grey sweatpants. I'd never really studied this man from the back, which meant, I'd never really noticed his rear. I wasn't normally a butt girl, but this guy had me changing my mind.

The way his muscles strained against his sleeves as he raised the pan to rinse it under the running water flooded my mind with thoughts of running into him this morning, shirtless and still wet from the shower. This man was sexy with and without clothes. My mouth turned dry, and I tried to swallow, but it was in vain. I felt like a fish on land.

What was I doing, standing here admiring this man? It wasn't like I was a free woman. I wasn't that kind of girl. I had so much going on already, and I needed to keep my head on straight or I was going to drown. The last thing I wanted to do was take this innocent, unsuspecting man down with me. I straightened my shoulders and pushed thoughts of shirtless Boone to the darkest corners of my mind.

"I'm gonna head out," I said, a bit too loud. When the sound made it back to my ears, I winced.

Boone didn't stop what he was doing. Instead, he just glanced over his shoulder in my direction. My heart picked up speed when I saw his mouth part slightly and his gaze glide up and down my body. My cheeks flushed as he brought his gaze up to meet mine. I wanted to believe that there was a hint of desire behind his dark blue eyes, but I didn't dwell on that thought.

It was ridiculous to think that a man would want me and my mess. Especially when I was carrying the child of another man.

No. To Boone, I was just a paycheck. He was transient. He'd made it clear to me that he had no intention of making Harmony his home. And there was no way I was leaving. Entertaining thoughts of a relationship with Boone was ridiculous, and I couldn't afford to be ridiculous.

"You look beautiful." Boone's voice came out low as he reached over to turn off the water and then faced me fully.

My heart fluttered at his compliment. I glanced down at my dress, my hands swishing against my skirt making the fabric dance around my legs. "Thanks," I whispered. Kevin rarely complimented me, and if he did, it was when he was six beers in and I was standing in front of him naked. Then it would be something crude that I would force myself to justify as he yanked me closer to him.

He never looked at me the way Boone was looking at me right now.

To Boone, *I* was beautiful. Fully clothed. Standing in front of him. No promise of anything physical. I was just...beautiful.

His pure affection scared me. I dropped my gaze from him and stared at the ground, hating how uncomfortable I was with his praise. It was too much.

"I should get going," I whispered as I walked over to the door. Once I was standing on the mat, I slipped on my shoes and then reached for the door handle. But before I could grasp it, Boone's hand beat me to it. Not wanting to look up at him, I kept my gaze focused on the door in front of me.

"I'm sorry," he whispered.

From the corner of my eyes, I saw him study me. "It's okay," I said. I glanced over at him and smiled. "I just don't want to be late."

His gaze searched mine as if he were looking for an answer to the question that I didn't want him to ask. "Do you want me to come with you?"

My entire body froze. "What?"

"I can come with you."

Was it wrong that I wanted him with me? He was on the only person on this entire Earth who I felt I could trust. And I wanted a trusted friend sitting next to me as Kevin stared me down. I knew I was going to refuse his offer, but that didn't mean I wasn't going to entertain what it would feel like to say yes.

"It's just dinner," I said, forcing a smile once more.

Boone paused, his eyes searching mine before he dropped his hand and stepped back. "Okay."

"I'll be back later." I grabbed the door handle and pulled it open.

I held my breath as I walked onto the porch. I forced my feet down the back steps. The gravel crunched around my sandals as I made my way to my car and unlocked the driver's door. It wasn't until I was buckled and the door shut that I finally let my breath out.

I shoved the key into the ignition. As I was backing out of the spot, I let my gaze slip back to the house. Boone was standing on the porch now. He'd stopped at the top step, his arm lifted and resting on the pole next to him. He was staring at me.

I couldn't read his gaze but I didn't try that hard. After all, I wasn't sure I had the strength to reject his offer if he asked me one more time.

Just as I drove past him, I waved. He didn't move, which made me wonder if he'd seen. I thought about turning around to do it again, but then decided against it. I didn't want to come across as desperate or weird, and turning around just to make sure Boone saw that I waved to him would put me solidly in the middle of crazy town.

Besides, I was on my way to see Kevin. I needed to

remove all thoughts of Boone and focus on the situation that I was about to walk into.

By the time I got off the island and to the restaurant, I'd forced all thoughts of Boone and the interaction between us from my mind. I exited off the freeway and into the largest city closest to Harmony, Athens. Leave it to Kevin to insist that we dine off the island. He always said he couldn't imagine himself eating anywhere that didn't have a Michelin star.

I almost went the wrong way down a one-way but, thankfully, corrected myself before driving into oncoming traffic. The restaurant had a valet, and I was more than happy to turn my keys over to the young man in a suit sitting behind the valet stand.

I smoothed down the front of my dress, wondering if I was underdressed, before I gathered my confidence and made my way to the front doors of the restaurant. This was what I wanted to wear, and if it wasn't good enough for Kevin, I wasn't going to care. I was done working to please that man.

The maître d' seemed to know who I was because he said Kevin's name before I could even speak. All I could do was nod. He extended his hand and beckoned me to follow him. I started to lead the way until I realized I didn't know where I was going, so I held back long enough for the maître d' to get in front.

Kevin was in the farthest table. He was sitting alone with a glass of wine in front of him. He was watching something on his phone, and when we approached the table, he didn't bother to look up. Instead, he silently clapped his hands before pumping his fist in the air.

I knew those gestures. He was watching a football game.

"Hey," I said as I stepped up next to him. I waited for him to get up to assist me with my chair, but he didn't even acknowledge me. I was left standing there, waiting for the gracious maître d' to help. He pulled out the chair and then helped me scoot it forward until I was comfortably sitting with my knees under the table.

"Good game?" I asked as I leaned forward, hoping that Kevin would see me.

"The Tigers are going to the Super Bowl," he said as he moved his phone like he was turning it off, but instead he just moved it so it wasn't directly in front of him...but it was still playing. "I'd put a million on that right now."

If I still cared about Kevin, his inability to give me his full and undivided attention would hurt. But not now. I'd gotten used to being his last priority.

His gaze drifted over to me before he leaned in and pressed his lips to my cheek. "You look beautiful," he whispered, his voice turning raspy. In the past, that would have my heart pumping and my body warming to his touch. Today, it was taking all of my strength not to shiver and pull away from his closeness.

If he sensed my hesitation, he didn't acknowledge it. Instead, he just reached over, grabbed the silverware that had been wrapped in a cloth napkin, and shook it out. Then he leaned forward and gently placed the napkin on my lap. As he drew his hands away, his fingers brushed my legs.

If it had been anyone else, I would have chalked up that touch to a mistake. But this was Kevin. He didn't make mistakes. Everything was always calculated with him. And the math was always skewed toward Kevin getting what he wanted from me even if I wasn't willing to give it.

"This place is nice," I said, deciding the best thing I could do was play along. This was going to be our last dinner. I needed information, and that was it. I wasn't here to get back with him. I wasn't here to mend our broken relationship. I didn't even want a friendship. I just wanted to know if he was willing to be a dad.

And if he wasn't, I was walking away.

"Ma told me about it. Thought I'd treat my lady." He leaned in and pressed his lips to my cheek. Then he paused, inhaling deeply. "When are you coming home?" he murmured against my temple.

My instinct was to stiffen at his touch, but I forced myself to remain relaxed. He'd know that something was wrong if I didn't melt into his arms like I'd done in the past, and I didn't want him suspecting anything.

"I think we have some things we need to work on," I said as I turned to meet his gaze. He was inches from my face. All I wanted to do was throw up, but I forced a smile instead.

He frowned. "Like marriage counseling?"

Like divorce. I wanted to say that aloud. I wanted to

speak it out to the universe. I wanted Kevin to hear it so he knew that we were over. But my tongue felt heavy in my mouth, making my ability to form the words feel impossible.

"Something like that," I finally managed to whisper.

Kevin frowned as he sat back in his chair but kept his arm draped on the back of mine. I could feel him staring at me. Like he was trying to figure me out. I just kept my gaze focused on the table, channeling my anxiety into adjusting the silverware.

"What do you want?" He leaned forward and I could feel his anger start to build. "Is it a baby? Is that what you want?"

I swallowed, the sound of that word on his lips made my stomach churn. "No. That's not what I want." I gathered all of my strength and turned to face him. "I don't think bringing a baby into this will fix anything. Especially if that's not what you want." I held his gaze.

He didn't speak right away. It was as if he were searching my eyes for an answer. "Well, I want one." He plopped back against his chair. "There. I said it. I want a baby."

My whole body froze. My ears were ringing, and my brain was having a hard time catching up. "What?" I whispered. My voice sounded far away and muffled. As if I were underwater.

Kevin took a sip of his wine. "I've just been thinking about it, and maybe I was too hasty in the past. I know back then I didn't want kids, but I'm getting older. It sounds nice." He shrugged as he set his glass down on the table. "I thought you would be happy about that."

I swallowed, unsure of what to think or say. Him wanting a baby was a huge step. It was something that I never thought I would hear him say. "I am happy," I said.

He glanced up at me and smiled. "So you want to have a family with me?"

That wasn't what I was saying, but I knew that he wouldn't take too kindly to rejection. So I just smiled for a moment, then my smile faltered. Was he saying he wanted kids as a ploy to get me back? If he was going to be in this child's life, I wanted him to really *want* the baby.

"Kevin..."

His eyebrows went up, and I could see his jaw muscles clench. I needed to be careful with what I was about to say.

"I think we should try to get some help first before we discuss bringing a baby into this world." There, that was diplomatic. It wasn't taking him back, but it wasn't forcing him away. If he wanted to be a father, I didn't want to be the kind of mother that stood in his way.

He reached forward and enveloped my hand with his. He leaned forward, his expression softening as he stared at me. "I love you, Juniper. I've missed you so much. You know I would never intentionally hurt you, right? You're the woman I'm supposed to be with." He brought his other hand over and slipped his fingers under my chin. He tilted my face so I was forced to look at him.

"Say you forgive me," he whispered as he held my gaze.

I knew buried somewhere inside of him was the man that I fell in love with. The man who would never hurt me. The man who would stay up late at night, laughing and joking with me. The man I would make love to until we were both sweaty and breathless.

I wanted to believe that that man still existed. If not for me and our marriage, then for our child. And I knew the moment I rejected him, that man would disappear forever.

So I said the three words that I didn't really believe but that I knew would preserve our relationship for a few more weeks. The three words that would give me time to digest what he said tonight. The three words that should only be spoken if they are truly meant. They felt like a bitter lie on my tongue.

"I forgive you."

10

BOONE

SWEET TEA & SOUTHERN GENTLEMAN

I threw my blanket off my body as I stared up at the dark ceiling above me. I'd been attempting to sleep for the last two hours without any luck. Now, I was very aware that it was eleven o'clock at night and Juniper was still not home.

Dammit.

I scrubbed my face with my hands, hoping to remove the image of her standing in that godforsaken dress in the kitchen with her hair framing her face and her pink, plump lips accenting her pale skin.

It had taken all of my strength not to hurry across the yard, pick her up, slam her car door, and bring her back to the house. I didn't like that she was going out with Kevin. I didn't like that I wasn't there, making sure she was protected. And I didn't like that despite her desire to be strong, I could still see the fear in the back of her gaze. The fear that I saw so many times in my mother.

The fear that had my muscles so tight they felt like springboards confined only by skin.

Unable to lie on the couch anymore, failing to convince myself that all I had to do was close my eyes and sleep would come, I sat up and shifted so that my feet were solidly on the floor. I leaned forward, resting my elbows on my knees as I dropped my head down. I closed my eyes and allowed the tightness in my neck to relax.

I needed to get out of here. This wasn't good for me. There was something about Juniper that was pulling me in, and I was becoming powerless to stop it. She was so goddamn beautiful and fragile. The way she stared up at me, begging me to protect her...it was feeding a part of my soul that ached to protect something so innocent.

She was good. I was not. I'd deluded myself into thinking that if I protected her, that would somehow redeem me. That all I needed to make myself right with my past was to be her knight in shining armor.

At least, that was how it started. Now, I could feel a shift inside of me, and it was a shift that I wasn't happy with. I was rapidly becoming aware that my reaction to Juniper wasn't only about protecting her. It was becoming personal.

I liked her. And I was beginning to like her a little too much.

I cursed under my breath as I stood and made my way into the kitchen. I'd taken off my shirt—it felt like it was strangling me—and all I had on were the grey sweatpants I'd worn earlier. I scrubbed my face with my hand and then pushed it through my hair. I blew out my breath as I opened the nearby cupboard and grabbed a glass.

I was done trying to pretend to sleep. I wasn't going to rest until I knew that she was safe and sound in her bed. I needed her to be here, where I could stand between her and anything that tried to harm her. Only then would I finally be able to relax.

I downed the glass of water and filled it again. After I turned off the faucet, I grabbed the full glass and a nearby magazine before making my way to the dining room table. I pulled out the chair that was nestled in the corner of the room. This allowed for maximum visibility of the kitchen.

I mindlessly flipped through what I could only assume was Mrs. Godwin's home decorating magazine, every so often stopping to stare out the open living room window with the hope that I could somehow will headlights to appear on the road.

Headlights that belonged to Juniper.

In my sick and twisted head, those headlights meant she was coming home to me instead of staying with her husband. I cursed under my breath as I turned my focus back to the picture of a bedroom spread in front of me, which was only half registering in my mind.

I was ridiculous. If I had any respect for Juniper and her family, I would walk away right now. Mr. Godwin asked me to protect her, and the thoughts that were invading my head right now were the furthest thing from keeping that promise.

Lights from the living room window snapped my focus

over. I waited, willing those lights to pull up the driveway. I watched as the car slowed and then took a right before pulling up next to the house. I wanted to stand and walk out the door just to see her get out of the car. I wanted to make sure that she was okay. But I knew if I did, she would know that I cared.

And I didn't want to care as much as I did.

So I forced myself to stay seated, staring down at the magazine, but the words and pictures weren't registering. My body was frozen as if any movement would pull my focus from Juniper. I would wait for the sound of the lock releasing and the door opening, then I would look up.

The headlights clicked off, causing the window to darken. I could hear murmuring, but I couldn't make out what words were being said. Was Juniper on the phone? Was she talking to herself?

My ears strained against the silence as my thoughts raced. Had she brought Kevin back?

My stomach sank as that question ping-ponged around in my head. Why was she back with him? And why would she let him back into her home?

The front door opened, and I heard Juniper's soft voice. "Good night, Kevin." My hands fisted at the sound of his name. So he was here.

"Come on, baby. It's been a while. Just let me in."

My jaw clenched. It was taking all of my strength not to go over there and show Kevin how I felt about him. I wanted to show him how I thought men like him should be treated.

"It's late and I have to be up early to get the store opened." She let out a soft giggle, but I could tell from the sound of her voice, she was nervous.

And I hated that.

"But you said your parents aren't here. You're alone. What would it hurt?" His voice got louder, which meant he was pushing his way into the house. "It's not like we haven't done it before." His laughter caused my muscles to flex. "We're pretty good at it." His voice was definitely closer now.

If he came in any further, I was going to have to move. I was going to intervene if he thought all he needed to do was say a few pushy words to get what he wanted.

"Boone's here." I closed my eyes, hating that my heart pounded at the sound of my name on her lips.

"Boone?" Silence. "That idiot from the diner?"

"Shh. Shh. He's probably sleeping right now."

"You're alone in your house with some random stranger? Let me talk to him." The sound of his voice growing louder had me pushing the chair away from the table as I stood.

Suddenly, he appeared in the doorway between the living room and the kitchen. His gaze snapped to me, and his cheeks turned red. I stood there, waiting to see what he was going to do. From behind him, I could see Juniper trying to rise up onto her tiptoes to see around his shoulder.

"He's my dad's guest." She wrapped her hand around his arm and attempted to pull him back.

She was like a fly on his windshield. One yank from his arm and her hand was dislodged.

"I think I should know the kind of man staying alone with *my wife*," he said, spittle flying from his lips as he spoke. He narrowed his eyes and rounded his shoulders.

My head cleared, and all I could see was Kevin. There was a likely chance that I was going to have to fight this man, and I was ready for it. Sure, I might get stuck in my head thinking about Juniper, but when it came to war, I was ready.

I was always ready.

Juniper's wide eyes and panicked look as she tried to catch my gaze snapped me from my focus. She looked scared, staring at me like she was trying to speak without saying a word.

She was worried, and I wasn't sure if it was for me or Kevin. Part of me hoped it was for Kevin. That she knew I was strong enough to physically push this man from the property. But I couldn't be sure. And that wasn't a theory I wanted to test.

I channeled my lessons in hostage negotiations and turned my focus to deescalating the situation. Juniper didn't want a brawl. She wanted Kevin to walk away safely. Even though that wasn't what I wanted, I was aware enough to realize that this wasn't about me. It was about her.

It was rapidly becoming all about her.

"Listen, man. I'm here because Ric—Mr. Godwin

wanted me here. That's all," I said as I raised my hands in a show of surrender.

Kevin's eyes narrowed as he flicked his gaze down to my bare chest and then back up. "Do you normally go shirtless around another man's wife?"

I felt Juniper's gaze on me. I wanted to look over to read her reaction, but there was no way I could break eye contact with Kevin. He needed my full and undivided attention. "I was just sleeping. It was hot so I took off my shirt. I don't normally walk around shirtless when I'm a guest in someone's home." I glanced over at Juniper; her expression was hard to read. "Right, Juniper?"

"He's normally fully clothed," she managed out. Her cheeks flushed as she glanced up at Kevin.

For a split second, I wondered if she was remembering our encounter this morning when she ran into me in the hallway. A smile threatened to show on my lips, but I fought it. "I have no intentions with your wife"—I spat the word out like it was something bitter in my mouth—"I just want to keep my promise to Mr. Godwin and help out around here until they get back."

Kevin didn't respond right away. Instead, he just stood there, staring me down. Seconds felt like hours as I waited for him to respond. Suddenly, Juniper's hand softly landed on Kevin's forearm, drawing his gaze over to her.

"There's nothing going on between Boone and me. I promise," she said, her voice hushed as she widened her eyes and looked up at him.

Kevin's body stilled. I could see the internal wrestle going on inside of him. Finally he stepped forward, wrapped his arms around Juniper, and she went crashing into his chest. My hand flexed as I watched him bury his face in her hair.

"I'm so sorry, babe," he murmured almost so low that I couldn't hear it. "I just miss you and seeing you with another man brings out this jealousy in me." He tipped his face forward and kissed the top of her shoulder. "I just want you home with me."

Juniper's body was tense, and it took her a moment to register Kevin's touch. I thought she was going to fight him off—at least I hoped she would—but she didn't. Instead, her arms went around him and she patted his back a few times.

"I know," she whispered as she stared straight ahead. "But it's for the best if I stay here...alone."

Kevin pulled back and looked down at her until he sighed and nodded. "If that's what you really want."

She met his gaze. "It's what we need."

He pulled her close once more, pressing his lips to hers. The anger inside of me was near boiling as I watched their interaction. I knew I should have pulled my gaze away, but I couldn't. I wanted to will my strength to her. I wanted her to tell him to leave and never come back.

She was worth so much more than what Kevin was willing to give her. She had to know that.

But instead of pulling away, repulsed, and declaring

their marriage over, she broke the kiss, took a step back, and folded her arms across her chest as if she were trying to protect herself. "Goodnight, Kevin," she said softly.

He stared down at her before flicking his gaze over to me. He sighed as he turned and made his way to the front door. "I'll text you tomorrow," he called over his shoulder. He yanked open the door and then pulled it shut behind him.

Silence filled the space between us. I glanced over at Juniper, wondering if she was going to speak. I had so many questions to ask her, but I couldn't seem to speak any of them. She looked so small and fragile, standing there in the doorway. Her gaze was unfocused as if she weren't really looking at anything, just thinking.

I parted my lips, ready to ask her if she was okay, but she spoke first. "I'm going to bed," she whispered as she turned on her heel and disappeared down the hallway.

She was gone. I was left staring at the space she'd once occupied, hating myself for all the words I couldn't find the strength to say.

I grabbed my glass of water and brought it to the sink. After washing it, I set it in the drying rack and wiped my hands on the dish towel hanging from the stove. I paced a few times as the desire to walk down the hallway and knock on her door began to grow out of control.

I wanted—no needed—to know if she was okay.

The desire grew too strong for me to ignore, so I growled

and headed toward her room. I stood in front of her door with my hand raised, ready to knock. I wanted to knock...

But I didn't. Instead, I dropped my hand and stared at the solid white door in front of me. I wondered what she was doing on the other side. Was she sitting on her bed? Was she crying? Was she happy or sad?

I wanted to know...no *needed* to know. But reality hit me like a semi sliding on a winding road of ice. She wasn't mine to know anything about. She was Kevin's. She was her parents'. But she wasn't mine.

And she never would be.

I closed my eyes and let my breath out slowly. Then I whispered, "Goodnight, Juniper," before I turned and headed back into the living room, where I collapsed on the couch. I pulled the blanket up over my face and stilled my body.

I was going to stay here until sunlight crept through the blinds. Even if I couldn't sleep, it didn't matter. I would stay here until morning because if I didn't, I feared my resolve to keep Juniper at arm's length would snap, and I would act. And if I acted, there was no way I would come back from it.

Staying at the Godwin's was the best thing that could have happened to me, and I would be a fool to mess that up. Mr. Godwin saved my life, and I was going to return the favor. Whether or not my heart wanted something different, it didn't matter. I had a debt to pay and nothing was going to stop me.

Not even the soft-spoken, doe-eyed beauty sleeping a few rooms away.

I was going to get a handle on my feelings if it was the last thing I did. Juniper wasn't mine. And she never would be.

11

ELLA

SWEET TEA & SOUTHERN GENTLEMAN

I slid my key into the door handle and turned. My entire body felt heavy from exhaustion as I pushed into my apartment and let the door swing shut behind me. I let my purse and computer bag slide off my shoulder into a pile at my feet.

After I got back from Harmony Cove, Gloria had me write up the article and then proceeded to spend the rest of the afternoon correcting it for me. I'd never had her so involved in a story of mine in the past. By the time 5 o'clock rolled around, I was physically and emotionally drained.

I was ready to change into my pajamas and curl up on the couch with a bag of chips and a fuzzy blanket while I binge-watched FRIENDS.

I yawned as I kicked off my heels at the door and then padded through the living room to my bedroom. I unzipped my pencil skirt and let it fall to the floor. I didn't bother picking it up as I unbuttoned my blouse and slid it off my shoulders before tossing it on the armchair in the corner of my room.

Thankfully, I'd done laundry over the weekend. I pulled my pink silk pajama bottom and top from the basket and dressed.

My body was already relaxing as I made my way into my bathroom and grabbed a scrunchie from the top drawer. I fashioned my hair into a messy bun at the top of my head before turning on the faucet so the water could warm up.

With my hair up and my face washed, I was beginning to feel more awake. I flipped off my bedroom light and headed into the kitchen. My watch vibrated on my wrist, and I glanced down to see that Asher had just texted me.

My stomach tightened at the sight of his name. Everything about the Harmony Cove deal, Gloria's refusal to let me write the article by myself, and the mystery man who told me to watch out for the Proctors was weighing on me. I couldn't shake the uneasy feeling I got when I was around anyone connected to Marcus Proctor. I was frustrated that my best friend—my *only* friend in Harmony—had aligned himself with that man.

I knew I couldn't ignore Asher's texts. He'd send a search party to come find me, and then I would have to explain myself to him. I'd have to tell him why I didn't answer when I was not dead in a ditch somewhere.

I didn't fully understand what was wrong with me, and

there was no way I would be able to articulate how I was feeling to him.

I walked over to the door where I'd left my purse. I fished out my phone and swiped it on.

Asher: Are you still at work, or did you slay the dragon?

He ended his question with a few emojis. I smiled. If he were here, he'd be pretending to draw his sword from its sheath and cut an imaginary dragon.

My friend was a dork and I loved it. But at the same time, I hated that Marcus Proctor was making me doubt the one constant man in my life. And I hated even more that I couldn't talk to Asher about it.

Me: The dragon has been conquered, and I am now at home, enjoying my spoils.

Asher only took seconds to respond.

Asher: Chinese. Fifteen minutes. We need to celebrate.

I parted my lips to complain, but then I closed them and shook my head. Even if I told Asher that I was tired, he wouldn't listen. He was coming over whether I wanted him to or not. So I just sent him a thumbs-up emoji and made my way back into the kitchen, where I set my phone on the counter and opened the fridge.

I was sitting on the couch with my fuzzy blanket wrapped around me like a tortilla, watching a FRIENDS rerun, when there were three knocks on the door. I tipped my face toward it and started to yell, "Come in," but the door opened before I finished.

Asher appeared in the doorway, carrying a drink tray and a white plastic bag full of Mr. Cheng's Chinese cuisine —our favorite.

"Hey," he said, his smile so wide that it made me angry at myself for being skeptical about his association with Marcus Proctor.

If his client had been anyone else, I would be jumping for joy. I wanted only good things for my friend. But I couldn't shake this nagging feeling in the back of my mind that something wasn't right.

And I hated myself for it.

Asher shut the door behind him and then turned. He crossed the space between us and set the bag of food and the drink tray down on the coffee table in front of me. "I got honey shrimp, chicken lo mein, egg rolls, and fried rice," he said when he turned to meet my gaze.

My salivary glands instantly activated. Asher was eyeing me, waiting for a response before a smile slowly spread across his lips. "If we're celebrating your success, why did you get everything that I love?" I asked as I untangled myself from my blanket before tossing it to the side and standing. The smell of the food made my stomach growl as I made my way into the kitchen to get plates and utensils.

Asher shrugged. "It all sounded good when I got there, so I just went with it."

I eyed him as I pulled two plates down from the

cupboard and then slid open a drawer and found two sets of chopsticks.

"So, what are we celebrating?" I asked as I bumped the drawer closed with my hip.

Asher studied me for a moment as if he were trying to figure me out. "The sale with Ms. McDonnell earlier today. You know, the one you *came* to."

I plopped down on the couch before setting a pair of chopsticks down on one of the plates and handing it over to Asher. "That's what I figured, but I was just making sure." I forced a smile. "So it really happened, huh?"

Asher dropped down on the couch next to me. I'd already pulled the little white boxes from the bag and was in the process of opening the honey shrimp. After I'd dumped some onto my plate, I realized that Asher hadn't moved, so I turned to see him sitting there, watching me.

I frowned as I licked some of the sauce from my fingertips. "You okay?" I asked.

He blinked a few times as he straightened as if he hadn't noticed that he'd been staring at me. "Yep, mm-hmm," he said as he leaned forward, resting his elbows on his thighs. "Sorry, I just zoned out there for a second." He yawned. "I'm wiped."

I nodded in agreement. "Me too."

"Gloria kept you that long?"

I shook my head. "Not longer than normal, but she was over my shoulder the whole afternoon. You'd think I was writing a piece on the president of the United States." I leaned forward and opened the next container. I dumped some of the chicken lo mein onto my plate and then set the container back down on the coffee table.

Asher picked it up as soon as I set it down and grabbed his chopsticks before he settled back on the couch. He proceeded to eat from the container, and I returned to opening the rest of the boxes. I had so many things I wanted to say to him. Questions I wanted to ask. But I wasn't sure how to say any of them without coming across as critical of my best friend's success.

"Barbara seemed excited," I finally said after I'd finished filling my plate. I grabbed the plate and chopsticks and leaned back on the couch.

I could feel Asher's gaze on me. "Yeah, she did."

I slipped some honey shrimp into my mouth, wondering what I was going to say next. Thankfully, Asher picked up the conversation. "It's a good thing. Ms. McDonnell sells her property for over market value, and the community gets a facelift. It's a win-win."

I pushed the fried rice around on my plate. "Why would the Proctors offer so much? Why not just offer market value?" From what I'd heard of the Proctor family, they weren't generous. I couldn't imagine they were out offering more than market value because they wanted the residents of Harmony to be wealthy. A business like that would get shut down so fast.

Asher didn't respond right away, and I paused before I glanced over at him. He was studying me, his gaze darker than I'd expected. He was chewing thoughtfully until he sighed, leaned forward, and placed the container of food on the coffee table.

"You know, I really didn't think it was my place to ask Mr. Proctor why he's doing what he's doing with his business."

There was a bite to his tone that surprised me. I'd struck a nerve. I hadn't meant to, but I'd made my friend upset. I needed to backtrack and fast.

"I'm sorry," I said, offering him a soft smile. "I guess never-ending questions is a hazard of the trade." I reached out and rested my hand on his arm. I never wanted to upset him. I wanted to be happy for him, I just couldn't shake the feeling that something weird was going on. I was worried about my friend and the community around me.

There was something wrong with the Proctors, and even though I told myself not to care, I couldn't stop myself. From the look on Asher's face, he knew that as well.

"This a good thing for me, Ella," he said as he straightened. "I wish you would just be happy for me."

I set my plate down and nodded. "I am," I said quickly. "I am happy for you. I want you to have success. You're my friend."

His gaze snapped down at me, and for a moment, I saw frustration flash in his eyes. Then he sighed. "Then be my friend."

I nodded. "I'm trying. I just..."

There was a battle going on inside of me. Should I say

what was truly on my mind, or say what I knew would salvage my friendship with Asher? I didn't want to lose him, but I also couldn't lie. That wasn't who I was.

"I don't trust the Proctor family. Something doesn't feel right, and I think you know that too." The truth tumbled from my lips before I could stop it. The man in front of me wasn't the Asher I knew. I couldn't understand why he wasn't even a little bit skeptical about all of this.

Sure, Ms. McDonnell had a nice house in a nice location, but for Mr. Proctor to come in and offer over its worth seemed strange. Why wasn't Asher seeing that?

"I gotta go," Asher said, suddenly standing. He grabbed the chopsticks that were sticking out of his lo mein and headed into the kitchen.

"Asher," I said as I hurried to follow after him, ""don't be mad at me." I could feel the dam of our friendship breaking, and I was worried that nothing I could say or do would stop that from happening.

"I'm not mad at you," he said as he dropped the chopsticks into the sink and turned.

I hadn't anticipated him turning around, and suddenly I was running straight into him. My hands sprawled across his chest in an effort to catch myself. Asher's arms went around my body, and his low voice whispered, "Whoa," so close to my ear that it sent shivers across my skin.

We stood there, frozen, in that embrace. The seconds seemed to slow as I tipped my gaze up to meet his. He was staring down at me with a dark, stormy gaze. I hated that I'd hurt my friend. I should have been supportive. I should have kept my mouth shut about my suspicions. *That* was how a true friend acted.

"I'm sorry," I said as I drew my eyebrows together so he could see that I felt bad.

He studied me before he sighed, dropped his arms, and took a step back. "I know." He pushed his hand through his hair. "I'm sorry, too." He shrugged. "I guess I just wanted you to be as excited as I was." In that moment, I hated myself. I hated that I couldn't turn off the reporter part of my brain. Not everything was a story. Not everything weird was untoward. For all I knew, the man who confronted me a few days ago was a disgruntled ex-employee who wanted revenge on the family. I had too big of an imagination sometimes, and I let stories run wild.

"I am excited," I said as I reached out and rested my hand on his forearm.

His gaze snapped down to where I was touching him before he slowly brought it up to meet mine. He looked conflicted, but I wanted him to know that I was still his friend. That I would support him no matter what. My issues weren't with him, they were with the Proctor family.

I pulled my hand away and snapped my fingers. "I have an idea," I said as I turned and started walking toward my bedroom.

"What?" Asher called after me.

I raised my hand and waved away his question. "I'm going to get ready," I said as I shut my bedroom door and headed straight into my closet to pull on a black crop top and a pair of high-waisted jeans. Once I was dressed, I put on a bit of makeup and pulled my hair out of the bun and brushed it before I pulled it back into a ponytail at the base of my neck. Then I slipped on a pair of Converse and headed out of my room.

Asher's eyebrows went up when I entered the living room. He was sitting on the couch with his arm draped across the back, scrolling on his phone. "You look nice," he said.

I warmed under his approving gaze. "Obviously," I said as I struck a pose and then walked over to where I'd dumped my purse. "Come on, let's go to Harmony Pub. We're going to celebrate the huge deal you closed." I turned the door handle and pulled the door open.

Asher looked skeptical before his smile widened and he moved to stand. "I could go for a drink," he said as he slipped his phone into his back pocket.

"Yeah you could!" I cheered and patted his back as he walked through the door.

I joined him in the hallway and then turned and locked my apartment door. I threaded my arm through his and held tight as we started walking toward the parking lot together.

I pushed all thoughts of Harmony Cove, the Proctors, and the legit deals they may or may not be making with the residents of this small island town from my mind. I felt my body relax when I laughed at Asher's jokes as he drove to the pub. Our conversation felt familiar as he pulled into the parking lot and turned his car engine off.

We walked side by side across the gravel. The music and conversations were equally loud as I followed Asher into the pub. We spent the evening laughing with Abigail and Shelby who'd come in for a girls' night out then I bought a drink for everyone in the pub and toasted to Asher.

He beamed at me as I raised my glass, and for the first time in a long time, I smiled. It was genuine because I was truly happy for my friend. I was going to enjoy this night of pure support because I knew tomorrow, no matter how much I tried to fight it, that nagging feeling at the back of my mind was going to return.

Tonight, I was celebrating Asher because I loved him. He was my best friend and he deserved to have this night. But tomorrow I would be back on the case. I was never going to forget about the mystery man or what he said about the Proctors. I was going to figure out the story behind that family, and I wasn't going to stop until I got answers.

I just hoped it wouldn't ruin my friendship with Asher in the process.

12

JUNIPER

SWEET TEA & SOUTHERN GENTLEMAN

I didn't know what to say to Boone when I woke up the next morning. I didn't know what to say while we both sat at the table eating breakfast. And I didn't know what to say while he drove us to the store.

Thankfully, he didn't try to talk to me and just let us sit in silence. I offered him a few soft smiles here and there, but that was the extent of our morning conversation.

When we got to the store, I focused on opening the registers, and Boone kept to himself as he went in and out of the back room gathering things to stock the shelves. Today we needed to go through the produce and get rid of anything that was expired. I was glad that he had a busy task ahead of him. It meant the chances of us needing to talk went down significantly.

It wasn't that I thought he'd done anything wrong. In fact, it was the opposite. *I* felt embarrassed for how Kevin acted last night. I was embarrassed that I'd allowed Kevin to barge into my parents' house like that. I felt embarrassed that I was standing next to the man Boone knew I was upset with. If I'd been stronger, Kevin wouldn't have walked all over me.

Last night was just another representation of how weak I was, and Boone got a front-row seat to that show.

I wanted Boone to think I could take care of myself. But last night when Kevin stepped up to him like he was looking for a fight, Boone had studied me, and I could see in his gaze the understanding that I was never going to be able to walk away from Kevin. That had been hard to see. I wanted my family and friends—and Boone was rapidly becoming a friend—to have confidence that I could make the right choice.

After last night, I doubted Boone felt that way.

I sighed as I pushed the drawer back into the register after filling it with the starting cash. I grabbed a spray bottle and some paper towels from under the register and began cleaning the glass on the scanner and then moved to wipe down the belt.

Eight o'clock rolled around, so I grabbed the keys and hurried to the front to open the sliding doors.

There was a steady stream of people today, which I was grateful for. It helped keep my thoughts at bay. There was a moment there when the line for my register spilled into produce. I moved to page Boone, but he'd already come to open another register. Once we made our way through the customers, he closed his register, nodded at me, and headed back to produce.

I was sitting on Mom's stool, reading a magazine, when he walked up to the register at noon. I hurriedly moved to stand, my head pumping as his gaze trained on me. Was this the time? Did he want to talk about Kevin?

"Hey, Boone," I said so quickly that it came out as a squeak. I swallowed hard, frustrated that I couldn't seem to get myself together.

He studied me for a moment before he tapped the conveyor belt for the register behind me. "Just wondering if you want me to take over so you can get some lunch."

Lunch. Of course. What did I think he was here for? My cheeks flushed with embarrassment, but I just nodded, hoping he hadn't noticed. "Yes. Of course." I set the magazine down under the register. "Lunch would be great."

He gave me a small smile as he moved to the side so I could get out. My shoulder brushed his chest, and for a moment, I thought I felt him tense. But when I finally found the courage to look at him, he seemed unfazed as he made his way into the register alcove.

I peeked over at him two more times as I hurried to Sal's meat counter to grab a sandwich. Thankfully, Boone didn't notice. He kept his gaze forward and focused on something else. When I brought back my lunch, which consisted of a sandwich, Doritos, and an apple, he rang me up in silence.

I thanked him, but he just nodded and leaned against Mom's chair, not once meeting my gaze. Regret settled in the bottom of my stomach when I realized that I may have just ruined our friendship. Boone was here to support me, and I'd gone and ruined it all by inviting Kevin back into my life.

Somehow, my relationship with Kevin made Boone upset, and I hated that. Boone was the only person in this small town who knew about the baby. That shared secret endeared him to me, and if I'd upset him, I wanted to fix it.

I just didn't know how.

I finished my food while watching some reels on my phone. My body was tense as if it remembered what happened yesterday and was anticipating it happening again today. I wouldn't put it past Kevin to make showing up at lunchtime a habit. I just prayed he'd stay away. I wanted to make sure Boone and I were cool before Kevin came around again.

I grabbed my garbage and headed to the trash to dump it inside. I tucked my phone into my back pocket and made my way from the back room to the registers. Boone was helping a customer, and as I neared, I recognized her. It was the same woman from yesterday that had been flirting with him.

And from the way her body leaned toward his, she was back at it again today.

Anger boiled in my gut as I approached. Was this woman never going to take the hint? Before I came into view of Boone and the woman, I saw her reach across the credit card machine and hand Boone a small piece of paper. I froze. He took the note and tucked it into his front pocket.

Her smile was way too big, which could only mean one thing—she'd just give him her number.

I don't know why, but that thought made me want to vomit right there on the grocery store floor. Which was stupid. Boone was a free man. He could date whomever he wanted. Why was I so upset that he was exercising that freedom? At some point, Boone was going to leave. I knew that, though the thought left a hollow feeling in my stomach.

Just because my life was a tangled and matted mess and happiness felt out of my reach, that didn't mean Boone should be stuck with me. If I were a true friend, I would be celebrating his relationship success. Whatever this weird angry feeling was, it needed to leave right now.

I was going to be happy for my friend even if I didn't feel it.

So, I forced a smile and approached the register. "Lunch was great. Thanks for taking over, Boone."

Boone snapped to attention, and his gaze whipped over to me. He looked like a kid caught with his hand in the cookie jar. Which was strange, but I just brushed it off.

"I'll take over from here," I said as I turned my attention to the woman Boone had been talking to. She was watching me with her eyebrow quirked like she was trying to figure out who I was.

I was more than happy to introduce myself. "I'm Juniper. My parents own this store," I said as I reached out my hand.

"Meaghan," she said, taking my hand.

"Nice to meet you, Meaghan." I pulled my hand back. "Are you getting to know Boone?" I asked as I flicked my gaze over to him. Boone was staring at the counter, not meeting mine or Meaghan's gaze.

"I am," she said, her voice turning to sugar. My stomach churned.

"Are you new around here?" I asked. "I don't think I've ever seen you in the store before yesterday."

She nodded. "I just moved here from Michigan last week." Her gaze drifted to Boone.

"Ah." I leaned forward. "Well, welcome. I hope Harmony has been treating you well."

Her gaze remained on Boone as she nodded. "It has."

I glanced from Boone to Meaghan. "Well, is there anything I can help you with? Looks like Boone rang you up." I was trying to be happy for my friend, but that didn't mean I wanted to witness the start of their love story. I got the sinking suspicious that, to her, I was just the third wheel.

She flicked her gaze over to me. "Actually, I—"

"There's someone coming up, so if you're done..." I nodded toward the sliding doors and gave her a wide smile.

She narrowed her eyes before she sighed and nodded. She wrapped her fingers around the shopping cart handle. "Call me, Boone," she said before she started pushing her cart out of the way.

Boone just nodded. I peeked over at him to find that his gaze was still trained on the register. He looked like he'd done something wrong. I felt bad. He shouldn't feel ashamed for seeing Meaghan.

Mrs. Wolf started unloading her groceries on the conveyor belt, and the sliding doors shut on Meaghan's retreating frame. Boone turned to leave. I hated that I might miss my opportunity to tell him that I was happy for him, so I reached out and rested my hand on his forearm.

"Wait," I whispered. My gaze was trained on his arm. His entire body had frozen in front of me. I slowly brought my gaze up to meet his. "Will you wait until I'm done with Mrs. Wolf? I...I want to talk to you about something."

His gaze was dark and stormy, but he nodded. "Sure."

"Thanks." I held his gaze for a moment before I turned to ring up Mrs. Wolf's 20 cans of cat food, meat, apples, and cat litter.

Once everything was paid for, Boone helped her load it into her cart. She gave us a shaking, "Thank you," before she made her way out to the parking lot.

I was suddenly alone with Boone, and all the things that I wanted to say to him left my mind. He was studying me as if he were waiting for me to talk. I knew I should talk, I just didn't know what to say.

"Thanks for helping me with Mrs. Wolf," I said, feeling like a complete idiot. This wasn't what Boone was waiting for. Why couldn't I just say the right thing?

He frowned as he glanced toward the sliding doors. "Of course. My pleasure."

I pinched my lips together as I nodded. I wanted to tell

him that I was okay with him dating Meaghan without making it sound like he needed my permission. But I couldn't figure out how to say it. I was going to melt under his gaze if I didn't say something soon.

"Meaghan seems nice," I finally blurted out.

Boone blinked a few times before he nodded. "She is nice."

"She eats a lot."

He drew his eyebrows together. "She does?"

What was I saying? I waved toward the store. "I mean, she came in here two days in a row. One can only deduce..." I needed to stop talking. Right. Now.

"Ah. She just moved into her apartment and realized she forgot to pick up aluminum foil yesterday. That's why she came back today." He folded his arms across his chest and leaned against the register as he studied me.

I felt like an idiot. Why did I have to open my big mouth? If I had a lick of sense, I would bid Boone a happy lunch and turn around. I would stop trying to suss out how he felt about Meaghan and if he was seeing her.

I would let my friend find his happiness.

I wanted to, anyway. It must be my pregnancy, but all my sense left my head as soon as I saw how Meaghan was looking at Boone.

"Do you have a big date planned with Meaghan?" I asked as I leaned toward him. "I saw her give you her number." As soon as the words were out of my mouth, I realized that the confession made me sound more like a stalker than just a curious friend.

His eyes widened. "Um, she just gave it to me after she told me about her art show this weekend. She wanted me to go to it."

"Oh." *Don't ask. Don't ask, Juniper.* "Are you going to go?"

His gaze felt like it was boring a hole into me. I could tell he was trying to figure out my intention. "I guess it depends on you."

My heart began to pound, and I felt my cheeks flush. "Me?" I whispered, surprised by my reaction.

He nodded. "I did promise your dad I'd watch over you while he was gone. If you need me here, I'll be here." His gaze intensified as if he wanted me to feel the weight of his words.

My first reaction was to tell him not to go. I wasn't sure about Meaghan, but I knew she wasn't right for him. I also knew it wasn't my place to ask him to stay. I hated myself for not being happy for him. These feelings were confusing me, and I shouldn't drag Boone down with me. If he wanted to go, he should go.

I scoffed and said, "I'll be fine." I forced a smile. "I'll probably just stay home and eat pizza and watch reruns. You don't need to be a part of that." I waved my hand at him to show how much I didn't need him around—even though I wanted him to stay.

He frowned. He was silent for a moment before he said, "You want me to go out with Meaghan?"

"Of course," I said, probably a little too quickly. I cleared my throat. "You're not going to live with us forever. Makes sense that you are finding a future." Then I hurried to add, "Or just testing the waters." I nodded. "It's good for you. I'm happy for you."

Those felt like the right words to say. I wanted him to know that I was supportive of his choices. He shouldn't be waiting around my parents' house. I knew he was new to town and probably needed a distraction. I wasn't the best of company right now, with Kevin hiding around every corner. I wanted Boone to find some peace, and I knew my situation wouldn't give that to him.

"So, you want me to go out on Saturday?" he asked.

"Of course."

We stood in silence for what felt like an eternity. I could feel Boone staring at me as if he were trying to figure me out. I gave him a wide smile before I turned and logged him out of the register and logged myself back in.

Boone didn't say anything as he walked past me. He didn't say anything as he came back to ring up his lunch of crackers and cheese. And he didn't say anything after lunch as he walked past the register and nodded at me to let me know that he was done.

His silence had my head whirling with thoughts as I spent the rest of the afternoon wondering if I'd said the wrong thing. Should I have told him that I needed him to stay? That I didn't want him to go? That thought confused me.

By the time I signed out of my register so Jordan could sign in, I still had no answers. Boone had managed to avoid having any more conversations with me. The only acknowledgement I got from him was when my line got too long again and he opened the far register to help. All he sent my way were a few head nods before he disappeared to the back.

"Do you have fun plans for dinner?" Jordan asked me, drawing me from my thoughts.

I startled and turned to look at her. "Huh?"

Her eyes widened as she studied me. "Dinner. Tonight. Do you have fun plans?"

Dinner. Memories of Boone wanting to cook me dinner rushed into my mind, and suddenly, I had a plan. "I have to go," I said as I hurried past Jordan.

I felt bad for leaving her there, sputtering at my retreat, but I needed to grab some ingredients if I was going to cook Boone dinner tonight. I had no plans to see Kevin—and I didn't want to. Boone wasn't going out with Meaghan until Saturday night. If I was going to fix the friendship that had blossomed between me and Boone, I needed to act.

I hurried through the aisle, grabbing stuff to make chicken Parmesan and spaghetti. Once my arms were full, I made my way to the register. I apologized to Jordan for leaving her so abruptly, but she just laughed and waved my apology off, saying she knew what it was like to have an ADHD moment. She was not offended.

I smiled and we engaged in small talk while she rang up my items. She asked me how my parents were doing, and I told her they must be busy because they hadn't reached out to me other than a few texts letting me know that they'd landed, they were with Aunt Christi, and they had a sea of doctor's appointments to take her to.

Jordan smiled and told me to wish them luck as she grabbed the receipt from the register and handed it to me. My hands were full, so I lifted my forefinger and thumb to take the receipt from her, and called a goodnight over my shoulder as I headed to the back.

I pushed through the swinging door to the back room and heard a "humph." I yelped and stepped around the door to see Boone standing there, rubbing his arm.

"Oh my gosh, I'm so sorry," I stuttered, my face flushing with embarrassment. I moved to set the bags down only to have Boone raise his hands.

"It's okay," he said as he bent down to meet my gaze. "I shouldn't be standing next to a swinging door." His fingers grazed mine as he moved to take my bags from me. "Here, let me carry these."

Electricity shot across my skin from the feeling of his skin brushing mine. My gaze snapped to his but he wasn't looking at me. I felt the weight of the bags leave my fingers as he slipped the handles off my hooked fingers. All I could do was breathe a soft, "Thanks."

He flicked his gaze down at me and nodded. "Of course."

"I want to make you dinner," tumbled from my lips.

His eyebrows went up.

"I mean, if that's okay with you."

He studied me before a soft smile spread across his lips. "It's okay with me."

My cheeks warmed as I whispered, "Great."

He kept a few inches behind me as I walked through the back hallway to the exit. I went to push on the door release, but Boone leaned forward, beating me to it. My shoulder brushed his chest once more, but instead of pulling back, I glanced over to see him staring at me.

His gaze was dark and unreadable. My lips moved in my effort to say something, but nothing came out. Instead, the smell of his cologne surrounded me, pushing out all rational thought.

I'm not sure how long we stood there, staring at each other, but he was the first to break the silence.

"Let's go," he said, his voice low and throaty. He pushed hard on the door so it swung open and I was able to walk through. He caught the door before it closed on me, and I waited just outside for him to join me.

For some reason, I wanted to be close to him. With Boone, I felt safe. Confused. But safe. And I wasn't ready to let that go.

Not tonight. And I had a sinking feeling, not tomorrow.

13

BOONE

SWEET TEA &
SOUTHERN GENTLEMAN

There was nothing more intoxicating than watching Juniper cook. In her baggy t-shirt and leggings with her hair cascading down her back, she was a vision, and I was hooked.

I was sitting at the peninsula with a glass of iced tea in front of me, watching as she moved around the kitchen, collecting bowls, utensils, and ingredients. Every time she stopped to drop something off on the counter in front of me, she smiled. I parted my lips to complain that I should really be cooking while she rested, but she beat me to speaking.

"Sit, Boone. You've cooked me so many meals, it's only fair that I repay the debt."

I wanted to tell her that there was no debt to repay. That I was honored to cook for her. That she gave me a purpose. She was my distraction. But I knew the moment I spoke those words, she would know what they meant.

I was falling for her.

Sure, we'd only known each other for a short time, but she was the air I breathed. She filled my thoughts every moment of every day. Being in her presence gave me the light I needed to continue. She was the puzzle piece that I was missing.

And I didn't know what I was going to do when the time came for me to leave.

Her insistence that I go on a date with Meaghan was like a dagger to the heart. But in a weird way, I was grateful she woke me up to my focus on her. After last night with Kevin, I needed to be prepared that she might go back to that loser. If distracting myself with Meaghan would make that hurt less, I would keep that bandage in my back pocket.

But that was a problem for future Boone. Tonight, I was going to enjoy it being just me and Juniper. No one else.

"Have you ever had chicken parm?" Juniper asked as she set the package of raw chicken down on the counter before removing a knife from the drawer and slicing open the plastic wrap.

I settled back on the barstool and folded my arms. "My mom made it once for her boyfriend..." My voice trailed off as I realized what I just said.

Juniper's gaze drifted to mine like she realized what I'd just said as well. Her lips parted before she smiled. I'd never mentioned my mom to her before. I dropped my hands to my legs and rubbed my thighs as I cleared my throat.

"Your mom?" she asked, her gaze turning tender. My heart pounded so hard I feared it would leap from my chest.

I cleared my throat again. "Yeah, my mom."

Juniper lowered the knife to the countertop and focused on me. "Tell me about her."

I wanted to tell Juniper everything. I just couldn't face the look on her face when she realized how I'd failed the one person I was supposed to protect. But her wish was my command. I would tell her anything if it meant she would continue looking at me the way she was looking at me right now.

"She was dating..." I paused as I tried to remember the deadbeat's name. "Ri—Rick at the time."

Her eyebrows went up as she returned her focus to the chicken. "At the time?"

"Yeah. Mom dated quite a few pieces of work growing up."

She was quiet, no doubt noticing the bite in my tone. It that came up every time I talked about the men who abused my mother. She had pulled the chicken breasts from the package and placed them in a bowl. Then brought them to the sink and turned on the faucet.

"And she made Rick chicken parm?" she asked as she turned to look at me while the bowl filled with water.

Her expression was so soft and inviting that all my previous anger and regret melted away. I didn't want to be that guy. I wanted to be the man she thought I was every time she looked at me.

"That would be a loose interpretation of what she did. The breading only stuck to one side, and she heated the oil so hot that it charred the chicken and set off the smoke alarm. She had to dump it in the backyard, and we drove to get fast food instead."

She laughed, the sound of her voice sent a rush of pleasure through my body. It was the best kind of music. "So, it was a bad experience," she said as she turned off the faucet and walked over to the paper towels and unrolled a handful.

"I'd say that." Especially since Rick came home drunk to find the house in shambles, and he beat Mom until she blacked out that night. But the time I spent with my mom at McDonald's was a happier memory.

Juniper turned her attention to the chicken and swished it around in the water. She held up a chicken breast and pressed it between her fingers so water dripped back into the bowl before she set it down on the paper towels she'd laid out.

She glanced over at me and I could tell that she wanted to ask me a question, but she wasn't sure if she should. "What?" I asked. I didn't want her to ask me about my mother, but at the same time I wanted to tell her everything.

She chewed her bottom lip as she narrowed her eyes. "Where is your mom now?"

I watched her, knowing that if I told her, there was no going back. She was going to have more questions and there was no way I wouldn't answer them. Maybe this was for the better. If she realized what I'd done, she'd walk away. From the way I needed to be around her, I knew I wouldn't be the one to leave.

"I—I mean, if you want to tell me." Her cheeks flushed as she returned her focus to the chicken. "You're an idiot, Juniper," she whispered to herself.

"She died."

Juniper's body tensed before she glanced over at me. "Oh, Boone. I'm so sorry. I shouldn't have asked."

I shook my head. "It's okay. I want you to know." The last sentence was out before I could police the words or lessen the intensity with which I spoke them.

My meaning wasn't lost on Juniper. Her body stilled as her gaze stayed focused on me. I held her gaze, wanting her to know that the words I'd said were true. I wanted her to know all the good things about me. I wanted her to see me with her goodness. I wanted to be the man that her and her family seemed to think I was.

I wanted it more than I wanted anything else in my life.

"How did she die?" Juniper finally whispered.

What did I say to that? The truth? Telling the truth would cause Juniper to pull far, far away from me. I couldn't stomach the look she would give me. I needed to hang on to her affection for a bit longer. "She got sick," was all I could get out.

Juniper's gaze turned sympathetic. "I'm so sorry. That must have been so hard for you."

All I could do was nod.

Juniper finished rinsing the chicken. She dumped out

the bowl of water and then began to pat off the chicken breasts. I enjoyed watching her, but hated myself for not being completely truthful. Mom had been sick, but it had been in her mind, not her body. Juniper probably thought she had cancer or something. I could have saved my mom if I'd been stronger, but I hadn't.

Her death was my fault.

"Well, I hope you enjoy this meal," Juniper said, tearing me from my reverie. She'd finished patting the chicken and was washing her hands.

"I'm sure I will," I said, offering her a smile.

She blushed and I loved the way her cheeks turned pink. She didn't respond as she moved to open the egg carton and pulled out an egg. She cracked the shell on the counter and brought it up over the small pie tin she'd pulled from the cabinet. She hooked her fingers inside the shell and pulled it apart.

Just as the egg and yolk plopped into the dish, she sucked in her breath. Her face paled and she dropped the shell into the egg. Her hand flew to her mouth while the other went to her stomach. She bent over and rushed from the room.

Without thinking, I was off the chair and following after her. As soon as she was in the bathroom, I heard the toilet lid open, and she was heaving into the bowl. My heart ached for her. I wanted to help, I just didn't know how.

She pushed her hair out of the way before her hand dropped to the ground and she heaved again. I stepped behind her and gathered her hair in my hands, pulling it off her neck. She made a small, whimpering sound—probably trying to tell me not to worry about it—but before she could protest, she returned to vomiting once more.

I stood behind her, holding her hair back until she finished and flushed the toilet. Her body was limp as she moved to lean against the tub next to her. I let go of her hair, and it fell around her shoulders as she closed her eyes and leaned forward to hold her forehead in her hand.

"I'm so embarrassed," she whispered.

I frowned. "Don't be."

She glanced up at me from between her fingers. "You just heard me puke." She closed her fingers and crisscrossed her legs so she could rest her elbow on her knee.

"Not the first time a girl has thrown up in front of me." Maybe boot camp didn't count, but I wasn't going to tell her that.

She peeked back up at me. "Really?"

I dropped down so I was at eye level to her, resting my elbows on my knees. "Really." I reached over and unrolled some toilet paper. Then I reached forward and started to wipe some of the throw-up that had gotten in her hair.

Her gaze followed my movement, and she sucked her breath in before pulling the toilet paper from my hand and quickly taking care of the rest. "Stop being so nice," she whispered as she leaned forward to throw away the toilet paper.

"Stop being nice?" I asked. I hadn't moved, and now that she'd straightened, she was inches away from me.

"Yes. Stop being so nice to me. I just threw up on myself, and you're taking care of me in a way Kevin never wo"—" Her voice broke, and she swallowed hard as tears filled her eyes.

I hated that that man hurt her like he did. She deserved so much better than what he was giving her.

"A way Kevin never would?" I finished for her.

She pinched her lips together and nodded. She looked so tired both emotionally and physically. I wanted to take care of her. I wanted her not to worry about her safety or the safety of the baby.

"Kevin's an ass," blurted from my lips.

Her eyes widened, and I wondered for a moment if I'd said the wrong thing—even if it was the truth. But I was right, and I was going to stick to it. I held up my hand to stop her protest. "You're carrying his baby. He should treat you like a queen. Hold your hair back, cook you dinner, carry you to bed..." My voice drifted off as I stared at her. "You should be the most important person to him."

Juniper was staring at me now. A tear slid down her cheek. I hated to see her cry. I reached forward and caught the tear with the tip of my finger. I brought my hand back, rubbing my thumb with my forefinger.

"I should shower," she said as she moved to stand, only to stop and grab her head like she was dizzy.

"Whoa, whoa," I said as I reached out to catch her if she needed it. "Just sit."

She nodded, wrapping her arms around her stomach and closing her eyes. "I get nauseous when I stand." She blew out her breath. "I'm looking forward to this going away in the second trimester. At least then I won't go walking around with throw-up in my hair."

Silence fell around us as Juniper kept her eyes closed. I glanced around, wondering if I should make the offer that lingered on the tip of my tongue. I used to wash my mom's hair in the sink when she was too weak to stand in the shower...I could do the same for Juniper. Feeling frustrated with my indecision, I decided to act. After all, it was my job to protect and take care of her. She was my one and only focus.

"Come with me," I whispered as I extended my hand for her to grab.

She eyed me before she slipped her hand in mine. "Okay," she whispered.

I helped her to stand before I wrapped my arm around her back and swept her knees up. I pulled her to my chest. "Let's go into the kitchen."

"Hang on, I need some mouthwash," she whispered as I passed by the sink. I set her feet down onto the ground but kept my hand around her back as she hurriedly tipped the bottle to her mouth, swished, and then spat it into the sink. She turned to me and smiled. "I'm ready."

She didn't ask questions as I carried her through the

house and into the kitchen. I sat her down on a chair next to the table, then moved to take care of the egg in the bowl. I got a container for the chicken and put it in the fridge. I figured she wasn't in the mood to eat quite yet.

After I cleaned the sink and cleared off the counter, I made my way back to her and offered my hand. She lifted her arm, and I picked her up once more and carried her to the sink.

I glanced down at her. "Do you trust me?" I asked, not sure if I wanted to hear the answer but praying that I hadn't overestimated our relationship.

She eyed me before she nodded. "Yes."

My heart surged, but I didn't linger on her response. I pulled her closer to my chest and lifted her high enough to clear the counter.

She squeaked. "Boone, what are you doing?"

I glanced down to see her staring up at me. Her eyes were so wide and trusting that my heart swelled.

"I used to do this for Mom," I said softly as I set her down on the counter next to the sink.

She drew her eyebrows together. "You used to do what?"

"My mom wasn't the best at picking men. There were a few who would abuse her. Once they left, she would be too weak to stand for a shower, so I used to wash her hair in the sink." I swallowed and closed my eyes as emotions rose in my stomach. "To get the blood from her hair."

Juniper took my hands in hers. "Oh, Boone," she whispered.

I opened my eyes to see her staring at me. I hated that she looked so sad when all I wanted was to see her smile. I reached out my free hand, and my fingers lingered next to her cheek before I mustered the courage to tuck her hair behind her ear. It may have been my imagination, but I swore she leaned into my touch.

"I'll be right back," I said, my voice low with emotion.

I slipped my hand from hers and made my way down the hallway to her bedroom. After gathering a few towels and the shampoo and conditioner from her shower, I made my way back to the kitchen. Juniper was still sitting on the counter, her legs swinging and her arms wrapped around her stomach as she stared at the floor in front of her.

I cleared my throat and her gaze snapped to mine. The smile on her lips made my heart soar. "Ready?" I asked.

She nodded. "Only if you are."

I made my way to her and set the items down on the counter. After fashioning a makeshift headrest next to the sink, I rested my hand on her shoulder. "Lean back."

She obeyed, scooting down the counter and then lying back as I held up her hair so it didn't get caught. I made sure she was comfortable before I dropped her hair into the sink. I flipped on the faucet and waited for the water to warm before I pulled the spray wand out and started to wet her hair.

"So, you took care of your mom?" Juniper asked.

Her eyes were closed and her eyelashes splayed across her cheeks. She was beautiful. I must have been staring too long because, a moment later, her eyes opened and she glanced up at me. "Boone?"

I snapped my attention back to her hair and cleared my throat. "Yeah, I guess you could say that," I said as I made sure that the hair at the nape of her neck was wet enough. My entire body was zapping with electricity from all the points of contact I was making with her right now.

"You were a good son," she said as she closed her eyes once more.

Her words felt like a dagger to my heart. As much as I wanted to agree with her—to believe that I was the man she thought I was—I couldn't. I knew the truth. I just didn't know how to tell her.

I returned the wand and grabbed her shampoo and lathered up my hands. I slipped my fingers into her hair and started to massage. The look of satisfaction on her face had my heart pounding. When she let out a soft moan, it took all my strength to keep my mind focused on the task at hand.

Thankfully, I finished soon and was able to rinse the shampoo from her hair. I took less time applying the conditioner, which really was a mercy move for myself. Once her hair was clean, I flipped off the faucet and squeezed the excess water from her hair. Then I grabbed a towel and wrapped it around her head.

I put my hand under her upper back and helped her sit up. She smiled at me once she was fully sitting.

"Are you sure you weren't a hair stylist in the past?" she asked as she tipped her head to the side and let the towel fall into her hands. Then she started working the towel down her hair.

"Nope, not a hair stylist." I dried my hands off with a nearby kitchen towel and then shoved them into the front pockets of my jeans.

She smiled as she nodded. "I know. Navy SEAL," she whispered.

I drew my gaze up to hers and nodded. "Yeah," I said.

"Well, thanks for this. I feel so much better." She set the towel down on the counter next to her and then moved to get off the counter.

Before I knew what I was doing, I closed the space between us, wrapped my arm around her waist, and slowly lowered her down onto her feet. Her hand went to my chest to steady herself, and I could feel her gaze. It was trained on my face.

"Thanks," she whispered.

Her feet were safely planted on the ground, but I hadn't let her go. Instead, I did the stupid thing and glanced down at her. The moment my gaze met hers, I realized that I never wanted to let her go. I wanted her to be mine.

"Of course," I whispered, hoping that she would understand just how I felt about her from those two words.

"I think I'll go get changed now," she said. She didn't pull away, instead, she smiled up at me as if she were waiting for me to let her go.

"Right," I said as I dropped my arm and stepped back. "Go, get dressed."

She nodded.

"I'll work on the dinner."

Realization passed over her face as she turned to me. "Oh, Boone, I'm so sorry," she said.

I shook my head. "Just go." I shrugged. "I like cooking." What I didn't say was, *I like cooking for you.* But that was the truth. She was the only person I wanted to cook for. The only person I ever wanted to cook for.

She nodded and walked over to the doorway that led to the hall. Then she stopped. "Thanks, Boone. Thanks for taking care of me." Her intoxicating eyes met mine as she smiled at me.

"My pleasure," I said.

With that, she turned and disappeared into the hallway, leaving me wondering what the hell I'd done and how I was ever going to walk away from this woman when the time came.

I was smitten. And if I didn't get out now, I doubted I would ever be able to.

14

JUNIPER

SWEET TEA &
SOUTHERN GENTLEMAN

I dressed in a new pair of leggings and a soft, worn t-shirt. I stood in front of the mirror in my bathroom, brushing my wet hair and staring at my reflection as I went over what had just happened with Boone.

He'd spent the last hour taking care of me more than Kevin had ever taken care of me in the years we'd been together. Kevin would have never held my hair back while I puked. If I'd thrown up in my hair and had been too weak to stand in the shower, he would have just handed me some wipes and told me to take care of it.

But not Boone.

His actions had me all sorts of confused.

For a moment, I allowed myself to think that this was how a man took care of the woman he loved, but then I wiped that from my head with a quick shake. Boone was not my man, and he certainly wasn't in love with me. He was just fulfilling his promise to my dad by taking care of me. That was all.

Still, I wanted to look nice in front of him, so I grabbed my mascara and swiped it across my lashes. Then I stared at myself, wondering if I was reading into things. I turned on the water and grabbed my makeup removing rag.

I studied my reflection in the mirror. I did look better with more pronounced lashes.

I flipped off the water. What did it hurt to *want* to look good? Unless he was the kind of guy who could tell when a woman was wearing makeup. Would he wonder why I was wearing it?

I turned the water back on.

Cursing myself, I turned the water off, squeezed the water out of my makeup rag, and set it next to the sink before flipping the bathroom light off and entering my bedroom. If I didn't get out to the kitchen, Boone was going to start wondering what was taking me so long.

I fluffed my damp hair as I pulled open my bedroom door and padded out into the hallway. Boone was busy in the kitchen. The smells of basil and tomato wafted past my nose and my once queasy stomach was grumbling with anticipation.

I couldn't fight a smile, so I gave up as I walked into the kitchen and found Boone standing near the stove. Steam was rising from various pots and pans in front of him. He had a pair of tongs in his hand and was busy flipping the breaded chicken.

"This smells divine," I said as I made my way toward the stove and peered over his arm.

"Careful," he said, using his free hand to stop me from getting too close. "This oil is popping tonight."

I glanced down to see five breaded chicken breasts in the pan. The crust was perfectly browned and only made my mouth water more. "Is it almost done?" I asked, fearing I might eat this entire house if he told me no.

He chuckled. "Have a seat at the table and I'll bring it as soon as I can."

I pouted but nodded and obeyed. I sat down on the dining room chair and got lost in watching him move. He was something I'd never expected, and I wasn't sure how to read him. He took care of his mom, but he was also a Navy SEAL. The man could cook in a way that would make Gordon Ramsey bow down, but he had a stare that said with one simple movement he could break your neck.

It was a strange combination, but Boone was slowly growing on me. It made me sad when I reminded myself that he was going to leave. Or date *Ms. Meaghan*.

I was a mess.

"Did your mom teach you how to cook?" I asked before my thoughts truly went wild and I wouldn't be able to rein them in.

Boone glanced over his shoulder and shook his head. "Nah. Back when I was growing up, my meals consisted of boiled hotdogs and Hamburger Helper with no hamburger." He lifted the pan of oil and chicken off the stove and set it on a trivet. He started pulling the chicken from the skillet and placing them on a plate layered with paper towels. "I actually learned from a buddy in the service. He taught me to cook while we were deployed and needed a distraction."

There was so much to Boone's life that I didn't know. His mom. His time in the service. He was this complicated puzzle that I knew I should keep my fingers off of, but every part of me desired to see the final product.

"Do you miss it?" The question left my lips before I could stop it. I inwardly cursed as I pinched my lips to remind myself to keep my nose out of other people's businesses. My mother would die if she knew how far I was prying into Boone's life.

He paused, his gaze turning thoughtful before he glanced over at me and said, "Every day since I left."

I wondered if I was supposed to respond, but as he continued, I sat back and listened.

"The service gave me something that I could never find at home. It gave me a family. It gave me a sense of belonging. And I was able to save people, unlike..."

His voice trailed off, and before I could stop myself, I whispered, "Your mom?"

His gaze slowly drifted over to me before he swallowed and nodded. "Yeah," he whispered.

The harsh beep of the kitchen timer cut through the tension. Boone snapped to attention and finished pulling the chicken Parmesan from the pan and then turned back to the pots still simmering on the stove. Five minutes later, he had our plates full of spaghetti and chicken Parmesan slathered in red sauce that had my mouth watering.

He brought me my plate with a fork and then returned with a large glass of ice water. Once he was certain that I was taken care of, he made his way back to the counter, where he grabbed his full plate and joined me at the table.

I was so hungry that I didn't notice the silence between us as we sat and ate. The food was almost as good as the scalp massage he had given me earlier. It wasn't fair that he had such an advantage over me. I didn't like being indebted to other people, even though I knew that he wouldn't come to collect. I wanted our relationship to at least be fifty-fifty, though I didn't know how that was going to happen.

My stomach was bursting by the time I finished, and I was grateful that I had put leggings on. I set my fork down next to my plate and stretched back with the hope to give my stomach just a little bit more room. But when I relaxed, my stomach felt just as smashed as it did before.

"I don't know what I'm gonna do," I said as I patted my stomach. "Someday soon it's not going to be a food baby taking up all this space, but an actual baby." My cheeks warmed as my words made their way back to my ears. Should I be embarrassed to talk about this with Boone? What was I saying? The man had already seen me throw up. It wasn't like we had a lot of secrets between us anymore.

"Are you nervous about having a baby?" Boone asked. He was scooping up the last remnants of spaghetti on his plate with his fork.

"Nervous?" I asked more for myself than for him. "I don't know." I glanced over at him. "Does that make me a bad mom? Not knowing how I feel about the baby I'm carrying?" I could feel tears prick my eyes. I didn't want to cry, but my hormones were already so out of whack that there was really no way to keep them in, even if I wanted to.

"I don't think it's possible for you to be a bad mom," Boone said, his voice so low that it rumbled from his chest. "I think if you love your child, that's all you need."

He was pushing around some crumbs on the table with his fingertips, and I could tell he wanted to say something more. I remained quiet.

"My mom struggled, but I always knew she loved me. And I think she was a great mom."

I reached across the table and rested my hand on top of his. "Of course she was a great mom," I said. "She raised a good son."

As those words left my lips, something changed in Boone. He pulled his hand back and straightened as if he had been poked by a hot iron. His gaze turned dark as he studied the table in front of him. "Don't say that." He had a bite to his tone that left me confused and wondering where I had gone wrong. "Please don't ever say that again."

Before I could ask him what I had said, or even apologize for having said the wrong thing, he was pushing his chair away from the table and gathering up the empty dishes. I was left sitting at the table, piecing through our conversation, while he busied himself with cleaning the dishes and loading the dishwasher.

I was so confused how this evening had gone south so fast. I complimented his mother. I complimented him. He had to know that he was a good guy. Right? He was a freaking Navy SEAL. The man had dedicated his life to saving others. How could he not see that he was an incredible person?

It couldn't be that. I must've said something that I didn't remember. Maybe if I gave him some time, he would come around. So, I decided to brush off his abrupt behavior and push out my chair. I joined him in the kitchen, where I grabbed a dish rag and rinsed it under the water that he had running for the dishes.

"You don't have to do that," Boone said as he approached the sink with the sauce pot.

"I think I do," I said as I turned to face him head-on. The scales were tipped in his favor, but I was determined to bring them back in my direction. Or at least bring them to equilibrium.

"You cooked dinner, it's my job to clean up," I said, staring him down as if to threaten him to speak.

"You're the one with the baby."

"So that makes me incapable of helping out?" I don't know if it was my frustration at the way he ended our conversation earlier or at his belief that I wasn't capable of helping since I was carrying a child. But I was ready for a fight if that was what Boone wanted.

He stared at me with his lips parted, like he was trying to process what I just said to him. He brought his eyebrows together as he started to shake his head. "I don't think you're incapable of helping out. I think you are a very capable woman."

It angered me that I couldn't even get him to fight me. This man had to have a flaw. It had to be somewhere in there, and for the sake of my sanity, I needed to find out what it was. If I didn't, I was scared that my feelings would continue to grow in the pit of my stomach. Every time I looked at him it would become unbearable. And when it came time to walk away, I wouldn't have the strength to do it.

"You need to stop doing that," I blurted out.

He frowned. "Doing what?"

"Being nice to me. Complimenting me. I know my dad asked you to take care of me and to help watch over his store, but I think you might be taking it a little bit too far." I squared my gaze with his. "Especially if you're not willing to let me return the favor."

"Return the favor?" he asked.

He couldn't possibly be this obtuse. "Earlier at the table, when I complimented you. You told me I had no idea what I was talking about."

It must have been the pregnancy. I would have never spoken like this to Kevin. But Boone frustrated and angered me in a way that had my thoughts spilling from my lips before I could stop them. It was refreshing and scary at the same time. I kept my thoughts buried when I was around Kevin because I knew how he would feel if I spoke them out loud. But I didn't know Boone. I didn't know how he was going to take it.

He leaned forward, and my first thought was that he was going to hit me. My entire body tensed as I flung my arms up to protect my face. The dish rag I'd been holding flew across the kitchen and landed with a wet sound. I closed my eyes tight, waiting for the first blow.

"Juniper?" Boone's voice was soft and near. "Why are you covering your face?" His voice broke like an emotional dam in his throat had ripped open.

I peeked over at him, and my entire heart felt as if it had been ripped from my chest. The expression on his face was one of horror as he stared at me. "I thought you were going to hit me," I confessed.

Boone closed his eyes for a moment, and his jaw muscles tensed as he digested my words. Then he opened his eyes and met my gaze with a force that I had never seen in a man before. "I will make you a promise that I will never break." He stepped closer. "I will never ever hurt you."

And I believed him. I dropped my arms from my face and nodded. "Okay," I whispered. "I trust you."

He studied me for a moment longer to make sure I knew that he meant what he said, before he turned to pick up the dish rag I had thrown. He brought it over to the sink and set it down on the counter before he opened the cupboard under the sink and pulled out a new one. He stuck it under the faucet until it was drenched, and then he rang it out before handing it to me.

I took it and he stepped out of the way. I walked over to the table and began to wipe it down, unsure of where to go from here. There had been something in his gaze. A desperation. Like he needed me to know that he would never hurt me in that way. Suddenly, my thoughts went back to what he had said about his mother and how he used to clean her up as a child. I closed my eyes for a moment and shook my head with frustration. If I had been stronger, I wouldn't have reacted that way.

If Kevin hadn't broken me, I wouldn't have thought Boone was going to hit me. All I felt was guilt and anger with myself.

"I'm so sorry," I whispered.

I glanced over at Boone to see him turn his face in my direction. He was frowning like he was trying to follow my words, but couldn't quite understand what I was trying to say.

"I said I was sorry," I repeated.

"For what?"

"For thinking that you were going to treat me like Kevin treated me." I stood there, my hand still holding the dishrag as it rested on the table.

Boone studied me for a moment before he turned off the water, dried his hands, and walked over to me. He was now standing inches away from me, his gaze intense.

"I'm a broken man, Juniper. There are things in my past

that you don't know. And I'm too scared to tell you because I'm worried how it will make you see me."

I parted my lips to speak, but he just shook his head.

"But even in my brokenness, I want you to know that *I* know you are worth so much more than what Kevin ever gave you. And if a man ever hurts you again, all you have to do is call me, and I will be there to take care of it. You will never have to fear again." He held my gaze as he let his last words linger in the air.

Electricity zapped between our bodies as he stared down at me. I knew what he was saying was true. I'd never been with a man so determined to make me feel safe. So determined to protect me. I was no one to Boone, and yet, he was offering to help me if and when I needed it.

Why wasn't Kevin that way? The man who vowed to love me in sickness and in health, for richer, for poorer.

For the first time in my life, I was getting a glimpse of how a man should treat me, and it was coming from a man who had been hired by my parents. I was confused and frustrated, but I knew one thing: I was never going to go back to Kevin if all he wanted was the status quo.

If Kevin wasn't willing to step up, there was no future between us. Boone had set a new bar for men in my life, and I was never going to be the same again.

15

ELLA

I woke up Wednesday morning to the sun creeping through my drapes. I stretched out my limbs, taking up every inch of the bed as I lay there, staring up at the ceiling. Today, I didn't have to be at work until noon because I would be staying late to get Sunday's articles formatted for the printer. I breathed out a soft sigh of relief. I had the morning to relax and rejuvenate, and I needed it.

Gloria had kept me exceptionally busy the last few days, and after my tense, dare I say, drama with Asher, every muscle in my body felt so tied up and tight that I was struggling to feel normal.

I was ready for a morning off so I could get my head on straight and my life back in order. I closed my eyes and requested Alexa to play my Saturday morning playlist. Soon, familiar music filled my room. I lay there, tapping my toe and singing along with the words.

Eventually, I rolled myself out of bed and padded into the bathroom to turn on the shower. Steam filled the space around me as I slipped out of my pajamas and into the hot water. I took my time washing my hair and shaving my legs. It was still warm in Harmony, and I was going to head to the farmers' market. No one wanted to see my hairy legs poking out from underneath the floral skirt I was planning to wear.

Once I was clean and smooth, I wrapped a towel around my body and one of Asher's old ratty t-shirts around my head—I'd taken it from his donate pile a while ago—and stepped out of the shower. I wiped the condensation off the mirror and stared at my reflection.

Thoughts of my interaction with Asher and Marcus Proctor were still stuck in the back of my mind. I wanted answers, I just wasn't sure how to go about getting them without completely offending Asher. I didn't want to ruin our friendship over something I wasn't completely certain about.

What if it turned out to be nothing? Was I willing to give up years of friendship with Asher for a potential story?

"You have to make sure there's something there before you blow everything up," I told my reflection, pointing my finger at myself so I knew to take myself seriously.

I'd always been so good at trusting my intuition. And Asher had always been so good at encouraging me to trust my intuition. This was the first time he'd asked me to stay away.

This was the first time my journalistic nature might hurt

someone I loved. And I didn't know how to juggle both things. I wanted to protect Asher, but also reveal the wrong-doings of someone closely tied to him. Thinking about it was causing knots to form in my stomach.

I shook my head. "The solution is to stop thinking about it," I mumbled under my breath as I flipped open my makeup bag and pulled out my foundation.

I went with a simple face today. After I blow-dried my hair, I turned off the bathroom light and made my way into my bedroom. I settled on a white shirt to go with my skirt. I dressed before I went back into the bathroom to curl my hair now that it had cooled.

I was finished and heading into the kitchen when my phone chimed.

Asher: You up?

I smiled even though his message made my stomach twist.

Me: Of course. Up and dressed.

Asher: Heading to the farmers' market?

I shook my head.

Me: You know me too well.

I set my phone down on the counter and busied myself with making some coffee. I grabbed a mug and a pod, and situated everything before I turned the machine on. Then I yawned as I rested my hip against the counter and waited.

Asher: Do you mind if your lifelong friend joins you?

I tapped the edge of my phone as I read his words. Normally, I'd love for him to come. But things were strained between us. Asher didn't feel any different—his text was proof of that—but I did. But if I rejected his request, he was going to ask me why. Did I really want to answer that?

"Ugh." I sighed as I rested my hands on the counter, dropped my head, and stretched out, closing my eyes. "Why is this so hard?" I moaned.

The coffee machine turned off. I straightened and removed my mug. I held it in both of my hands as I took a few sips. Maybe after I was sufficiently caffeinated, I would feel better. The answer to all of my problems would be made known.

After I'd drank half of my cup, I still felt conflicted. I glared at my phone like it was the problem before I picked it up and swiped it on. Asher's latest text stared back at me as if daring me to respond. I knew I couldn't leave him on *read*. I was going to have to respond at some point.

Right now was as good of a time as any.

Me: Sure! Sorry that took so long. I needed some caffeine.

I paused.

Me: Meet me in thirty?

Asher sent back a thumbs-up emoji. I clicked my phone off and set it back down on the counter. I drank the rest of my coffee and then rinsed the mug out in the sink. I dried my hands, grabbed my phone and my purse that was hanging on the wall. I pulled the strap up onto my shoulder as I pulled my keys from inside. Then I opened my apartment door and stepped outside.

The sun was shining and wind blew around me, smelling like salt and relaxation. I turned and locked the door before I headed down the stairs to the parking lot. I was so grateful when Asher found me this apartment. It was close to the water and the view was picturesque every time I stepped outside.

I climbed into my car and turned the engine on. Fifteen minutes later, I pulled into the town square and found a parking spot down one of the narrow streets. Just as I slammed the driver's door and moved to open the back so I could grab my shopping bag, I heard Asher's familiar voice. "Hey, Ella."

My insides twisted from the familiar cadence of him speaking my name. I felt guilty and annoyed at the same time. I forced a smile and straightened. "Hey," I breathed out as I found the strap to my bag and threaded my arm through it. "Have you been waiting long?"

Asher was wearing a pair of shorts and a black t-shirt. He looked so relaxed compared to his normal suit and tie. He shoved his hands into his front pockets and shook his head. "Nope. Just got here." He nodded toward his truck that was parked on the opposite side of the road.

I let my gaze roam over him before I frowned. "You don't have a bag." I narrowed my eyes. "If you think you're going to be using mine, you're sorely mistaken."

He chuckled as he shook his head. "Don't worry, I would never imagine asking you to share your bag with me." He shrugged. "I'm just here to spend some time with you."

His half smile made me feel even more guilty for how I'd been acting.

Asher was a good friend. Why couldn't I be the same?

"Well, just remember that you agreed to carry everything you buy," I said as I pointed my forefinger toward his chest.

He held up his hands. "I promise."

I narrowed my eyes one more time before I turned and started walking toward the town square, where farmers and vendors had set up. Asher fell into step with me. We walked in silence. I kept peeking over at him, wondering if I should say something and hating that I felt so awkward.

This wasn't how I was supposed to feel around him. He was my best friend. I was supposed to be relaxed and open with him. I feared that I was never going to feel the same again. Had I fundamentally changed our relationship?

"Have you had a good week?" Asher's voice broke through my thoughts. I turned to see him glancing down at me. He was asking me about my week? Had our relationship really dissolved to this level? Was he feeling it too?

I nodded. "It's been busy. I'm glad to have the morning off." I scoffed. "As long as Gloria doesn't call me in a panic 'cause we have to rewrite an entire story.

He laughed. "I wouldn't put it past her."

"Truth."

Silence. Again. This was its own level of hell. And I hated it.

"How about you? Did you close on any more properties?"

He shook his head. "It's been pretty quiet after my work with Mr. Proctor..." His voice trailed off as if he suddenly realized what he'd just said.

The silence turned awkward, and I was desperate to dispel it. "I'm sure that'll turn around. Lots of people are moving to Harmony."

He nodded. "Yeah. I have an open house later today. Hoping to get some bites."

"That's nice." I peeked over at him to see that he'd drawn his lips together as he stared at the ground. "Isn't it?" I asked, wondering if he was having an issue with that listing.

He glanced over at me and nodded. "Oh, it's nice. I can't imagine the house will stay on the market long."

"That's good."

Ugh. *That's good. That's nice.* Was this what our relationship had come to? I felt like I was walking on eggshells around him. He had to be feeling the same, 'cause I could feel the difference in our conversation.

We were standing in the middle of the square now, with booths all around us. Asher kept shifting his weight as he focused on everything but me, and I was doing the same.

"I should get some tomatoes," I said when I spied a table with an assortment of vegetables.

"Oh, okay." Asher hesitated and then followed after me as I started walking.

I chatted with the owner of the vegetable stand while I picked out small baskets of tomatoes, cucumbers, zucchini, and summer squash. He tallied up my total, and I handed him cash. While I waited for my change, I dumped each basket into my reusable bag and then handed the baskets back to him.

With my cash in hand, I turned to Asher, who gave me a soft smile before following me to the next booth.

I ended the trip with a bag full of vegetables and containers of local honey and homemade strawberry-rhubarb jam tucked between my arm and chest.

"You really didn't want anything," I said as I stared pointedly at his empty arms.

He shrugged. "Naw. I'm good."

"So, you came all the way to town just to watch me buy things," I said as I spotted my car and made my way toward it.

"Pretty much." He shrugged. "I didn't want you to be alone."

I glanced over my shoulder at him. Even if he felt like our relationship was strained, he was still determined to see me. Asher really was a good friend. *I* was the issue.

"Thanks," I whispered, hating the fact that I was never going to be as loyal to Asher as he was to me.

His phone beat him to a response. The ring cut through the silence between us. He held up his hand as he pulled out his phone. "Hello?"

I turned my focus forward, but from the sound of his

footsteps and the way his voice remained constant, I knew Asher was still following behind me.

"Hey, Collin." He paused. "I can do that." Silence again. "Yeah, I'll see what I can do about tracking him down."

I wasn't close enough to hear the other side of the conversation and I wasn't sure I wanted to. I had a sinking suspicion that this Collin character worked for Marcus Proctor, and the less I knew, the better.

"I'll head over there after my open house."

I was standing in front of my car now. I set the jars down on the hood before I fished my keys from my purse.

"I understand, but I have to—"

It seemed the man on the other end of the call was not happy with Asher's response.

"I do have other clients that I have to—" I peeked over at Asher. He had tipped his body away from me with his head dipped down as he held the phone to his ear. "No, I don't want that." He must have felt my stare because he turned his gaze to mine, and I saw worry in my best friend's eyes. "Yes. I'll head right over there."

Collin must have not even bothered to say goodbye because Asher didn't return the sentiment. Instead, he just shoved his phone into his back pocket. He gave me a forced smile as he nodded toward his car.

"I gotta go," he said as he started to back up.

I wanted to call him back. I wanted him to tell me what was wrong. I wanted not to care about who he was working for. I wanted to turn off my journalistic brain that always saw a story in every situation I got myself into.

I wanted to be a support to him. I just wanted to be his friend. But from the way he'd looked at me and the hushed tones he'd spoken in, I wasn't sure we were that anymore.

That's when I realized what was happening. I was losing my best friend.

And if I didn't stop him from slipping away, I was going to lose him. Forever.

16

BOONE

SWEET TEA &
SOUTHERN GENTLEMAN

It was five in the morning, and I was awake. In all honesty, I hadn't slept much last night. I'd spent most of my time tossing and turning. Thoughts of my night with Juniper haunted me in a sort of morbid fantasy.

I wanted to be the hero in her story. I wanted to be the man to save her and carry her away from the toxic situation with Kevin, but then the sight of her wide eyes and panicked expression when she thought I was going to hurt her crashed into my mind, grounding me back in reality.

Kevin may be the villain, but I was the monster.

I yanked my blankets off and sat up. I planted my feet on the ground in front of me while I rested my elbows on my knees and tipped my head forward. There was no way I was going to be able to fall asleep. And there was no way I could hang out here with my thoughts.

I needed to run.

I grabbed a pair of basketball shorts and a t-shirt and headed into the bathroom. Once I was changed and I'd splashed some water on my face, I opened the door and made my way back into the living room. I dug through my bag for a pair of clean socks, then laced up my tennis shoes and stood.

As soon as my feet were pounding the pavement and I was taking in deep breaths of salty air, my mind began to clear. I forced out all thoughts of Juniper and focused on the task at hand: running until I stomped out my feelings for her.

Last night was the first time I'd felt alive in so long. Touching Juniper. Feeling her body under my fingertips. Seeing her stare up at me with trust and admiration made me long for more. I felt like the Grinch. When Juniper was around, my heart grew.

I feared who I would become when I left.

I closed my eyes for a moment, focusing on the sound of my breath. *Inhale. Exhale. Inhale. Exhale.* I opened my eyes. I was running on the side of the road. Thankfully, in a small town no one was up this early, and I was alone on the road. The occasional car passed, but they were few and far between.

I ran and ran. I was going to keep running until I could accept that Juniper and I were never going to be what I so desperately wanted us to be. I wanted her to be mine. I wanted to protect her until my last breath.

But she wasn't mine, and she never would be.

Thirty minutes later, I glanced up to see the sign for Harmony Cove in the distance. I blinked, confused how I got here. I left not knowing where I was going to run to, and suddenly, my mother's community came into view. My body thought it knew what I needed while my mind remained oblivious.

I didn't stop when I ran past the weatherworn sign. I was just going to go until my body told me to stop. A left and then a right, and suddenly I was standing in front of mom's house for the second time since I'd returned home.

I stood on the sidewalk, my chest expanding as I tried to calm my breath and heart. I let my gaze drift over her house. I could hear her call after me as I stormed from her house and didn't look back. She was weak but stood her ground that she wasn't going to leave Bob. Her flavor of the week.

I was done trying to get her to see that the men she brought home weren't good for her. And she was done trying to convince me that I was wrong.

She spat out a slew of curse words before she told me to leave and never come back. I took her up on that offer. I just hadn't realized that conversation was going to be our last.

I closed my eyes and tipped my face up toward the sky. I'd give anything to go back and just hug her. Tell her that I loved her even if, in that moment, she hated me. To take her with me. Free her of the pain that came with every man who entered her life and left it.

As much as I hated my mom for not being strong enough, I hated myself more for failing her.

I tipped my face forward again and my gaze focused on the front door. The last time I'd come, I'd only been able to make it to the driveway. My feet started to move, and I walked from the sidewalk to the driveway.

The walkway to the front door was crumbling and littered with weeds. My steps felt heavy as I made my way up it and climbed the two steps to the front stoop. I pulled open the storm door and stared at the door handle.

I lifted my hands, my fingers brushing the metal. Was I strong enough to open the door? My fingers curled around the knob and I twisted it. It shifted but didn't turn fully.

It was locked.

I dropped my hand and glanced around. Mom always had a spare hidden outside the front door for me. I wondered if it was still there. I glanced around but didn't see the hide-a-key rock. I backed up and down the steps, keeping my gaze focused on the river rock in front of the house. There was a patch of weeds that had grown to my hip, so I pushed them down with my foot.

Tucked in the far back of that patch, near the house, I found the familiar grey rock that stuck out if you knew what you were looking for.

I bent down and picked it up. I rotated it, looking for the opening, and heard the key shifting inside. I pressed on the release, and the little door swung open. I could see the key nestled inside, so I tipped it into my hand.

I stared at the key as it lay on my palm.

Was I really going to do this? Was I going to walk into my mother's house?

I steeled my nerves and returned to the stoop. I held onto the key as I slid it into the lock and turned. I could hear the lock disengaging. It was a soft click. But with the way my nerves were feeling, it echoed in my mind. I stared at the doorknob now, knowing that all I had to do was turn it and push, and I would be inside my mother's house. Facing the past that I'd spent so long running from.

I lifted my hand, my fingers brushing the metal before they curled around the knob.

One. Two. Three...

I wasn't ready. I wasn't ready to face what was inside of this house. I wasn't ready to face the place I should have stayed.

I should have saved my mom.

My chest felt restricted as I reengaged the lock and pulled the key from the knob. I slipped it back into the hide-a-key and buried it deep into the patch of weeds.

I needed to get out of here. It was a mistake to come.

I hurried down the sidewalk and crossed the driveway. Just as I made it to the sidewalk, the sound of someone clearing their throat startled me. An older man was standing on the sidewalk with a curious terrier sniffing my shoes. The man's eyebrows were raised, and he was staring at me.

"Geez," I said, clutching my chest as I leaned forward to catch my breath. "You scared me."

"You from around here?"

I glanced up before I straightened. "Kind of."

He frowned. "What are you doing poking around Hannah Lewis's house?" He folded his arms. "I haven't seen anyone come or go from that house in years."

"I, um...er." I didn't know what to say. This man didn't seem to know that I was her son, and I wasn't sure I was ready for that information to get out there.

The man sighed, loud and pointed, while pinching the bridge of his nose and closing his eyes. "I'm going to be grateful when all you investment companies get the hell out of our small community." He opened his eyes to stare at me. "We just want to be left alone."

Did he think I was with the Proctors? My stomach churned. There was no way I wanted to be associated with those people. "I'm not—"

"I'll tell you this, you're wasting your time with that house. I'm not even sure her son can be reached and he's the one that inherited it." He pointed his finger at the house. "It'll be going up for auction soon. Apparently, Hannah's son hasn't been paying the property taxes on it."

I hated how he made me sound irresponsible. I wanted to defend myself to this man, but I also wanted to keep my anonymity. Besides, he did have a point. I *hadn't* been paying the property taxes. But I'd been busy, and back then, coming home was the last thing I wanted to do.

The man tsked as he brought his gaze from the house to me. "It's sad though. Hannah always waited for her son to come home. I know she'd be brokenhearted if she knew that he never came back before it was sold off." He shrugged. "That woman didn't have a lot, but what she did have, she was proud to leave to her son."

The vice around my chest tightened. Emotion coated my throat, and I feared that if I didn't get out of here right now, I was going to break down in front of this stranger.

I needed to get the hell out of here.

I dipped my head, thanked the man for his time, and jogged back down the street. It had been a mistake to come here. I should have stayed away.

Anxiety and regret filled my body, and I ran faster and faster to get them to leave. But no matter how fast I ran, I couldn't outrun what that man had said.

My mom waited for me to come home...and I never did.

My throat crackled with each swallow. I cleared my throat in an effort to remove the emotions that were built up inside, but nothing I did could appease my guilt.

I was sweating when I finally got to the Godwin's street. I didn't stop running until I was at the end of the driveway. I was panting as I leaned forward to catch my breath. I stared at the pavement, sweat dripping down my face.

My shirt felt like it was strangling me, so I straightened and, in one swift movement, pulled it off. I gripped the fabric as I turned my attention back to the house and, for the first time, noticed a black SUV.

I frowned as I approached it. Was Kevin here?

The driver's door opened, and a man stepped out. He was wearing a suit, and his hair was slicked back against his head. "Boone Lewis?" he asked as he stepped forward and extended his hand.

I glanced down at it but didn't take it. "Yeah."

He held his hand out for a few more seconds before he curled his fingers into his palm and dropped his hand. "Collin Baker. You're a hard man to get a hold of."

I snapped my gaze up to the Godwin's house. Had he knocked? Did Juniper know that a Proctor lackey was currently parked in her parents' driveway?

"What do you want?" I asked, praying that she was still asleep. I needed to get this man away from me. "I'm not selling."

Collin was in the middle of pulling something from the inner pocket of his jacket, but my words made him pause. He glanced up at me with his eyes wide. "You haven't even heard my offer."

I shook my head. "Doesn't matter. I'm not selling." I stepped to the side. "So, you can get out of here." I was done with him stalking me. This kind of behavior may work on other people in this town, but it wasn't going to work on me.

"Mr. Lewis. I suggest that you listen to this offer. I'm not sure you're going to hear it again. Besides, I've been to the courthouse. I know that the taxes haven't been paid." He leaned closer to me. "Very soon, you're going to lose the negotiating power you seem to think you have."

I didn't like this man, and I didn't like what he was implying. This was my mother's house, and there was no way I would sell it to a man who was most likely going to bulldoze it.

I held his gaze as I leaned into him. "I'm not selling," I said before I sidestepped him, crossed the yard, and went up the front porch steps.

My mind was racing and my ears ringing as I pulled open the front door and stepped inside. I pulled the door closed behind me and glanced up only to stop in my tracks.

Juniper was standing in the doorway to the kitchen. Her satin robe was open, exposing the short satin pajama set she was wearing. Her long, creamy legs had me swallowing. Her hair billowed around her shoulders, and she was carrying a mug in her hands.

Her eyebrows were drawn together. "Where were you?" she asked softly before she tipped her focus to the front window, which currently showed Collin pulling out of the driveway. "Who was that?"

I shook my head, not wanting to talk. My emotions were a wreck, and I needed a shower to clear my head. "Wrong house," I said as I made my way across the living room.

I could feel Juniper's gaze on me as I walked past her to the hallway. I felt horrible for brushing her off like this, but I wasn't ready to talk to anyone about what had happened at my mother's or the fact that the Proctor family seemed to think they could get what they wanted by harassing me.

They were pushing me, and I was a man who would not be pushed.

Juniper didn't respond, but I really didn't give her a

chance to. I shut the door on her surprised expression, pulled open the shower curtain, and flipped the water on. I planted my fists down on the vanity and tipped my head forward as I let steam fill the air around me.

I closed my eyes, hating that I'd started this morning out trying to clear my head, and I only managed to muck it up that much more.

I was a mess. And I was beginning to realize that, no matter what I did, I was going to stay a mess.

The last thing I should do was involve Juniper. Her situation was complicated enough, and I was being selfish wanting to stay around her.

If I was truly falling in love with her, then the best thing I could do was to walk away.

She deserved all the happiness in the world. And in order for her to have that, I needed to leave her.

Forever.

17

JUNIPER

SWEET TEA & SOUTHERN GENTLEMAN

My heart was pounding as Boone stood in front of me, shirtless and sweaty. I'd woken to find him gone. At first, I thought he'd left for good. But when I spotted his green, military-issued bag, relief filled my chest.

I'd had a hard time sleeping last night. My thoughts were full of what had happened the night before and how safe I'd felt in Boone's presence. It made me realize that this was what I was missing in my life. This was what I was missing in my marriage. I needed a man who made me feel protected.

I awoke, ready to tell Boone that I wanted to file for divorce, but he wasn't there. Now, he was standing in front of me with a dark, stormy gaze, his chest heaving in and out from his run. His hair was damp and fell across his forehead, and he looked like he'd just run into an old enemy.

"Are you okay?" When Boone didn't answer, I tried a

different question. "Where were you?" Movement by the front window drew my attention over. "Who was that? Do you know him?"

Boone dropped his gaze and shook his head. "Wrong house."

I parted my lips to inquire more, but Boone tipped his head forward and crossed the living room before I could get the words out. The sound of the bathroom door closing filled the silence.

I kept my gaze on the door, wondering what had just happened. I felt so connected to him last night. And seeing him come in and keep his answers short before making a beeline for the bathroom was strange.

Maybe I had misinterpreted everything last night.

Or maybe he really knew the guy that had parked in my parent's driveway. I glanced back to the living room window before I went to the front door and pulled it open. I watched as the SUV drove by and got a good view of the driver. He looked about ten years older than me. He had dark hair and glasses perched on his nose. He met my gaze before he drove off.

I watched him until he took a left and disappeared down the next street.

Who was this man, and why did he have such an effect on Boone? My stomach twisted. I didn't like not knowing what was going on. Kevin always kept things from me. He always left me in the dark, and I hated that. I didn't think

Boone was like Kevin, but I couldn't help but wonder if Boone had told the truth. Did he really not know this man?

I stepped back into the house and shut the door. I took the last few sips of my herbal tea—I'd done some research on coffee and pregnancy, and decided not to risk it—as I walked into the kitchen. After rinsing my mug and slipping it onto the top rack, I shut the dishwasher and started it.

I was ready for a shower.

I felt better when I stepped out onto my plush bathmat and wrapped a towel around my body. Steam had filled my bathroom, so I leaned forward and swiped my hand across the mirror. I stared at my reflection as reality hit me.

I was divorcing Kevin.

My life was fundamentally going to change. Was I ready for that? I narrowed my eyes as I studied myself.

It scared me. I would be a fool to say that it didn't. But I knew one thing for sure, I was ready. I was stepping out into the unknown, surrounded by darkness and uncertainty. And even though I feared what my future would look like, I knew it didn't involve Kevin.

I dried off and dressed. By the time I got back into the bathroom, the steam had dissipated. I worked on doing my hair and makeup. I gave my reflection a once-over before I turned off the light and made my way out of my room and down the hallway.

It smelled like cake batter and maple syrup when I rounded the corner and walked into the kitchen. Boone was standing next to the griddle with a spatula, flipping one of the pancakes in front of him.

"Smells amazing," I said, my stomach growling so loud I figured he could hear it.

He turned and smiled at me. "Morning."

I studied him for a moment. He looked calm. His eyes were back to their sky-blue color. His hair was damp, and he was dressed in a black t-shirt and jeans.

"Morning," I said as I moved further into the kitchen. I had so many questions for him, but I wasn't sure how to start asking any of them.

He turned his attention back to the griddle. "Did you sleep well?" He flipped another pancake.

I nodded. "I did."

"No more nausea?" He glanced over his shoulder at me.

"Not really."

Boone grabbed a nearby plate that had some sausage links on it. He added a few pancakes before handing the plate to me. "No eggs," he said, his lips tipping up into a smile.

The sight of the egg yolk and whites from last night flashed in my mind, and I felt my stomach tighten from the memory. I swallowed the saliva that flooded my mouth as I took the fork he'd extended to me and hurried over to the table. Food seemed to appease my nausea more than anything.

After slathering my pancakes with butter and syrup, I

dove in. When the food touched my tongue, I let out a soft moan. This was delicious.

"Good?" Boone asked.

I turned to see him watching me, but my mouth was full, so all I could do was nod.

He smiled. "Good."

He finished off the batter and dropped the bowl in the sink. He put together a second plate of pancakes before he joined me at the table with his plate and a mug of coffee. We ate in silence until my curiosity got the better of me.

"You were up early," I said as I cut off another chunk of pancake with the edge of my fork.

He glanced up at me and nodded. "I needed a run."

"I figured." This man was determined to remain cryptic to me. "The trails here in Harmony are amazing. Did you run along the shoreline?"

Boone paused before he glanced over at me. "Something like that."

This conversation was going nowhere. Not with Boone giving me three-word sentences. I wanted to push, but he was making it clear that he wasn't really interested in telling me where he'd been. So, I decided to shift topics. Boone already knew about the baby; he might as well be the first to find out about my marriage to Kevin.

"I think I'm ready." The sentence came out as a whisper. My chest squeezed with fear from just speaking the words, but I needed to be stronger than the fear. I needed someone to know what I wanted before I chickened out.

"You're ready?" he asked, turning his attention to me.

I nodded. "I'm ready. I'm ready to divorce Kevin." I was staring at the wood tabletop in front of me before I slowly raised my gaze to meet his. "My marriage is over."

Boone was quiet for a moment as he studied me. Then he nodded. "Okay."

I dropped my gaze back to the table and pushed around some crumbs with the tips of my fingers. "Do you think...you can help me?" I peeked up at him to see he was watching me.

He must have sensed my gaze, because a moment later, he raised his to meet mine. I felt like he was searching my gaze, and then relief filled my chest when he started to nod.

"Of course. I'd be happy to help."

I reached forward and laid my hand on his. I felt him freeze as he stared down at our hands before he glanced up at me.

"Thanks," I whispered, my throat tightening from emotion.

Boone had really gone above and beyond with his promise to Dad. He'd been present for this fundamental shift in the trajectory of my life. I wasn't sure what I was going to do when he decided that he was finished with Harmony, and I wasn't sure I wanted him to go.

He was the most constant thing in my changing life, and even though I'd only known him for a short time, he felt so foundational that I knew when he left, I was going to feel it.

And I wasn't ready for it.

We kept our conversation light for the rest of breakfast. Then we worked together to clean the kitchen and we drove to the store. He made me laugh as he recounted his time in the military as we readied the store. He took to the back as I prepped the register.

When the time came, I unlocked the sliding door and returned to the checkout lane. By midday, the store was bustling with people. I had a steady stream of customers but never really got backed up enough to have to call Boone to help.

It was eleven thirty when I saw a man about my age approach the register. He looked like a man on a mission as he caught my gaze and smiled.

"Hi," he said as he stood a few feet away from me, grasping his hands as he leaned forward.

I handed Mrs. Parkes her receipt. She thanked me and headed toward the sliding doors. I had no more customers, so I turned my attention to him. "Hello, how can I help you?" I asked, confused as to why he'd started his grocery shopping experience with talking to me.

"I'm looking for Boone Lewis, and I was told he works here."

I frowned.

The man seemed to pick up on my reaction. "Does he work here?"

"Um...who are you?"

He shook his head like he'd just realized he made a

mistake. "So sorry, I'm Asher Wolfe. I'm a new realtor on the island." He extended his hand.

I studied it before I took it. "Juniper Godwin." I pulled my hand back. "What does a realtor want with Boone?"

"So, he works here?"

Crap. Well, I'd already given up the game. But I wasn't just going to send this man back to Boone without sussing out who he was first. If he wasn't good for Boone, I was going to send him on his way.

"He works here, but I don't let anyone harass my employees." I stood straighter as I studied him.

Asher widened his eyes and held up his hands. "I'm not harassing him at all. I just wanted to run something by him."

I frowned.

"It's completely innocent, I promise." A silence fell between us. Asher must have realized that I wasn't going to give up his location, so he moved to pull his phone from his pocket. "I have a reference if you want. Ella Calipso. Do you know her? She's a journalist here on Harmony."

Ella. "You know Ella?"

He nodded. "You know Ella?"

"I've met her."

He laughed. "Then you know if I'm friends with her, then I can't be bad, right?"

I didn't know that, but if he knew Ella, then there was a certain level of trust I could give him. And maybe this was all innocent, and I was making a big deal out of nothing. I sighed before I narrowed my eyes and then nodded my head toward the back of the store. "Last I saw, he was stocking the ice cream freezers."

Asher flicked his gaze in the direction I'd indicated before he nodded. "Wonderful." He didn't acknowledge me again as he passed by in front of me and headed toward the freezers.

I sat at the register, stewing over what had just happened. What did a realtor want with Boone? I chewed on my thumbnail as my mind swirled with questions.

Had I done the wrong thing, sending that man to look for Boone?

Unable to stand at the register any longer, I picked up the phone and pressed four to ring the bakery. Kate answered after two rings.

"Hey, Juniper."

"Kate, can you do me a favor?"

"Sure."

As soon as Kate got to the register, I told her I'd be right back and headed to find Boone and Asher. I found them tucked in the back corner, with Asher talking and Boone listening. Thankfully, neither man noticed me as I approached.

"...I understand, but this is a solid offer on your mother's house that is struggling."

Boone was staring at the cooler in front of him. I could tell that he was listening, but from this body language, he wasn't happy with what was being said. Guilt washed over me. I should have sent Asher packing, especially if this was about Boone's mom.

"I don't mean to push you, but Collin is looking for an answer soon." Just as Asher finished speaking, his gaze flicked over to me.

That seemed to get Boone's attention, because a moment later, he looked as well. Now that I was found out, I quickened my pace. "You found Boone," I said as I stepped up to the two men.

Asher's smile was back, and Boone's expression was stone. Was he mad at me? "I did." Asher clapped Boone on the shoulder. Boone's entire body tensed, but Asher didn't seem to notice. "I appreciate you listening to me," he said as he stepped around Boone. "And I'll get out of your hair to let you think."

He flashed me a smile as he passed by and headed to the front of store. I was left standing next to Boone. I peeked up at him, worried that I'd created a wedge between us. He was determined to protect me. Shouldn't I have done the same?

"I'm so sorry. I had no idea what he wanted when he asked for you." I stepped closer to Boone. "I thought it was innocent. I didn't think it was about your mom..." My voice trailed off as Boone turned his body away from me and back to the cooler that he must have been stocking.

"It's fine. I'm not upset," he said as he pulled open the door and a blast of cold air surrounded us.

"I know, but I should have vetted—"

"I found a lawyer," Boone interrupted.

I stopped and stared at him. "You did?"

He nodded before removing a torn paper from his back pocket. "His name is David Phillips. His firm is in Powta, and he can see you Friday." I held out my hand, and he pressed the paper into my palm. "I told him noon would work." His gaze drifted to mine as he held my hand with his. "I'll cover for you while you go."

My gaze lingered on our hands before it slowly made its way to meet his. My heart was pounding as electricity zapped throughout my body. I never wanted him to let me go. I felt safe and secure when he was around, and I wasn't ready to lose that.

"Thanks," I whispered as I studied his gaze. Did he know what he was doing to me? That I wasn't going to ever be satisfied with another man again? Boone had shown me what it was like to be cherished. And I feared I would never be able to find that with anyone else.

He held my gaze. "Of course," he said. His gaze intensified like he wanted me to know something, but I was too scared to allow myself to guess what that was.

I wanted to stand next to Boone forever, but I knew I needed to get back to relieve Kate. So, I forced my feet to move, and I eventually got back to the registers. Kate asked me if I was okay, and all I could do was nod. She looked confused but hurried back to the bakery without asking more questions.

I leaned against the stool, my mind swirling with thoughts of Boone. Those thoughts made me more convinced that divorcing Kevin was the right move. I hoped we could move through the courts quickly. And when I was finally free...

I hoped that Boone would still be here.

My phone buzzed, drawing my attention over to the screen. Kevin had texted me.

I picked up my phone to see that he'd sent an invitation for lunch tomorrow with a location and time. My resolve to end our marriage grew stronger, so I pressed on the message bar and typed back.

Me: I'll be there.

18

ELLA

SWEET TEA & SOUTHERN GENTLEMAN

"Well, I'm out for the day," Gloria announced as she stood in her office doorway, pulling her purse strap up onto her shoulder. Her gaze settled on me because, in all honesty, I was the only one she was talking to.

Everyone else was headed out soon, leaving me alone to work on the articles for the Sunday edition. When I first started at the paper, I was honored that Gloria trusted me with this task, but then I realized it was just grunt work. She'd already decided which articles went on which page, it was my job to make it all fit.

It had bothered me at first, but then I began to look forward to Wednesdays. I got to come in late and spend the evening at the office by myself. I would order a hamburger and fries from the diner, drink some Dr. Pepper, kick my shoes off, and blare my music while I worked.

It was kind of perfect.

Elizabeth was the last one to leave. I followed her to the door while she told me about the fight she got into with her boyfriend the night before. As she neared the door, she stopped and turned to continue the conversation. I listened and nodded for a few minutes before I reached forward and pressed on the door release.

"It sounds like you're just going to have to talk to him," I said as the evening air surrounded us.

Elizabeth chewed her bottom lip before she nodded. "You're probably right." She smiled over at me. "You're such a good listener."

"Thanks," I said, still holding the door open.

She hugged her notebook to her chest before she took a step outside. "Are you sure you don't want me to stay? I can help."

I shook my head. "I'm okay. Plus, you really should go talk to Gus."

She sighed as she turned to the parking lot before she glanced back over to me. "You're probably right. I'll see you tomorrow?"

"I'll be here."

She smiled and then turned and headed toward her car. I watched to make sure she got in safely and then let go of the door. Once it was shut, I turned the lock and headed back to my desk.

I kicked my heels off and navigated to my playlist on the computer. I hummed along with the words to the first song as I opened the email Gloria had sent me and got started.

I'd only mapped out the front page by the time Tim knocked at the front door with my bag of food from the diner. I raised my hand so he knew I'd seen him as I pushed away from my desk and padded over to unlock and open the door. I stuffed a twenty and a five into his hand and told him to keep the change as I took the bag from him.

I let the door close behind me before I turned and locked it once more. I settled back down at my desk, unwrapped the straw, and poked it into the lid of my Dr. Pepper. I munched on the fries and burger while I worked. When I was finished, I leaned back in my chair and then bounced a few times as I studied the layout in front of me.

The paper looked good to print.

I yawned and stretched before I gathered my garbage and dumped it into my trash can. Just as I straightened, there was a soft tap on the front door. I paused before glancing over. Had I really heard a knock?

I shook my head and turned my attention back to my desk. I hadn't heard anything. It was just one of the curses of working alone at night. Every noise became someone or something.

I brushed the salt from my fingertips over the garbage can when the sound came again. This time, I couldn't brush it off as ambient noise. There was really someone at the door.

I pushed my chair back and stood before I made my way over. I unlocked the door and pulled it open only to see Mrs.

McDonnell standing there. She was wringing her hands as she glanced around behind her.

"Mrs. McDonnell?" I asked as I opened the door further.

"Oh, good, my dear. You're still here."

I nodded. "I'm always here this late on a Wednesday." I frowned. "Did you need something?"

She began rapidly blinking like she was trying to keep tears at bay. "Yes," she whispered. "I just spoke with Tim Turnbough from down the street. He's agreed to sell his property to the Proctors just like I did."

I reached out and rested my hand on her forearm. That seemed to do the trick. She pinched her lips as I glanced around. "Why don't you come inside?" I stepped away from the doorway and waved her in. She nodded and entered.

I locked the door once we were both securely in the room. Then I waved for her to follow me to my desk. I was fairly certain that Gloria didn't have cameras inside of the paper. Security cameras outside were another story.

I grabbed Elizabeth's chair and pulled it next to my desk and motioned for Mrs. McDonnell to sit. She obeyed, and I grabbed the arm of my desk chair and pulled it so it was facing her before I sat.

I offered her a small smile. "It's probably safer if we speak in here."

She nodded. "Of course." She took in a deep breath. "Tim came over to me not even an hour ago. I guess he just received word about the appraisal on his home."

"Okay."

She closed her eyes as if she were preparing herself to speak the next words. "He said that it came back at *half* what Marcus had offered."

My eyes widened. "Half?"

She nodded. "Half."

"Then don't sell."

Tears brimmed her eyes once more. "That's the thing. When Tim called the Proctors to inform them that he was pulling out of the deal, they told him there was a clause in the contract. He couldn't back out of the deal if there were factors outside of the Proctor's control." She began to wring her hands. "Appraisals are out of their control."

This stunk. This entire situation stunk to high heaven. Something was going on. I wasn't sure what it was, but my gut knew. It had always known. Even if this entire town seemed indebted to them, the Proctors were dirty.

I reached out and rested my hand on Mrs. McDonnell's. She glanced up at me. Her tears had been set free, and they were now running down her cheeks.

"I'm going to lose my home." Her voice was barely registering now. "And it's not about the money, I promise. But I was going to help my kids. If the appraisal comes in at half, I'll be left with next to nothing. I can't give them the legacy when I pass that their father wanted to give them." Her chin quivered. "I've ruined everything."

Anger and fury rose up inside of me. I shook my head as

I focused my gaze on her. She had to know that she didn't cause any of this. The Proctors did. Asher did.

Realization hit me like a ton of bricks. Asher had sat at that table and told her this was a good offer. He'd been instrumental in helping close this deal. Did he know that this was going to happen? Was he working with the Proctors to deceive these people?

Was this the reason he told me not to look into that stranger outside of the paper?

My emotions sat like a rock in my stomach. I was angry at myself for not listening to my gut. I was mad at Asher for making me doubt myself. And I was worried that my friendship was ruined. Because there was no way I could sit on this. I was going to bring it to the community's attention.

I had to.

"You didn't ruin everything. Let me look into this and get back to you." I smiled up at her. "They don't own your house just yet. There's still time."

My words didn't seem to be the salve I hoped they would be. Mrs. McDonnell just shook her head. "I wish I had your confidence, sweetie. But this is Marcus Proctor we're talking about here." Her voice dropped to a whisper once more. "I've already lost."

"No." I shook my head. "Give me some time. I promise, I will fight this. Proctor or not, they won't get away with this."

Mrs. McDonnell smiled. "Thank you."

"Of course."

I spent the next ten minutes going over every detail and writing down what she said word for word. I told her I would call her as soon as I discovered anything. I also told her to wait to see what her appraisal would look like. By the time she left the paper, she seemed to be in better spirits even if she was still doubtful that I could actually do anything.

I couldn't blame her. The grip the Proctors had on this town was one of near strangulation. And I knew they weren't going to let go without a fight.

I was in a reporter daze, just staring off and letting my mind wander, when my phone buzzed. I blinked, centering myself as I glanced over at my phone. Someone had just texted me.

Worried that it was Asher wondering what I was doing tonight, I almost ignored it. Until I remembered that it could also be Gloria. I picked it up.

The last thing I needed was Gloria thinking I couldn't handle the paper layout and come trouncing down here. I needed her to believe that I had everything under control so she would leave me alone. Especially since I knew where her loyalties lay, and they weren't with the truth.

But it wasn't Asher or Gloria who had texted me. It was Shelby. I frowned as I read her text.

Shelby: Some of us ladies are going out to Harmony Pub in about an hour. Wanna join?

Perfect. That was exactly what I needed. I didn't want to hang out here at the paper by myself. My mind would go crazy with questions and theories about the Proctors. And if I were home, I'd be doing the same.

Going out with a group of women all ready and eager to talk seemed like the perfect distraction.

I texted a quick thumbs-up emoji, and she responded with a smiley face. I put my phone down and focused on finishing up the layout before I saved it, closed my computer, and slipped it into my bag. I turned off the lights and pulled out my keys to lock up as I walked outside.

Once Harmony Gazette was all buttoned up, I made my way to my car and climbed inside. Shelby and Abigail were at the pub when I walked in fifteen minutes later. They'd grabbed a table in the back, and as soon as they saw me, they waved.

I nodded to them before I headed over to Jax and ordered a Diet Coke. He nodded, but it was Claire who told me she'd bring it over after she grabbed Shelby's iced tea and Abigail's glass of wine.

I thanked her and made my way to the table, where I pulled out a chair and collapsed on it.

"Busy day?" Shelby asked as she smiled at me.

"Long day."

"Gloria's working you that hard?" Abigail asked.

"Pretty much. I had to put together the layout for Sunday's paper. I've been there since noon." Not to mention my stress-filled, tension-packed morning at the farmers' market with Asher. This day felt as if it were going on and on.

I was grateful that it was at least ending this way.

"You need this more than me," Abigail said as she handed me the glass of wine Claire had just brought her.

I laughed and shook my head. "Only if I want a raging headache in the morning. I think that might not solve my issues."

Abigail smiled as she took a sip.

Shelby and Claire had engaged in conversation, so I turned back to Abigail. She was so nice, and I was grateful that I was finding friends in Harmony. "How are things with Bash?"

She was mid-sip, so she pressed her finger to her lips as she swallowed. "He's good. Busy." She sighed. "He's in so many negotiations when he is here, I barely see him."

"Negotiations?"

She nodded. "His company has been buying up real estate around the island."

I paused, my ears perking up. "Real estate? Like buildings or houses?"

She frowned like she was trying to recall. "I think both." Then she sighed. "I mean, I love that our little town is finally getting recognized for its beauty, I just don't want it to lose its old-time charm."

"I totally understand." I paused, my journalist hat landing solidly on my head. "I was in Harmony Cove this week, interviewing a resident who had just sold their house to the Proctors."

Abigail glanced over at me. "Oh, Bash has been telling

me all about that. He's been surprised at how expensive those houses are. I keep telling him that Harmony Cove is prime real estate." She sighed. "I wish my aunt hadn't sold her house back in the day. We'd be rolling in the dough if she'd held on to it."

"Bash said that Harmony Cove's houses are top dollar?" My ears were ringing.

She nodded. "Crazy high. Like, millions."

My mind was swirling. If Bash's company was buying up Harmony Cove houses for millions, but the Proctors were telling the residents the appraisals had come in low...I shook my head.

I needed to do some research. Ordinarily, I'd call the expert, but I had a sinking suspicion that my only expert wouldn't be too happy if I was moments away from ripping the curtain off a real estate scandal he was involved in.

I downed my soda and grabbed a twenty out of my purse. I set it down on the table and turned to the ladies, who were now all watching me. "I've gotta go," I said as I stood and pushed in my chair.

"I realized I forgot an article, and if I don't get the file to the printers by midnight, Gloria is going to have my head." I gave them a quick smile.

"Of course," Shelby said. "Do what you gotta do."

I nodded at them before I turned and hurried through the pub. As soon as I was outside with the front door swinging shut behind me, I took off jogging toward my car.

I didn't go home. Instead, I went straight to the paper

and unlocked the door. As soon as I was inside, I headed straight to my desk, grabbed my computer from my bag, and plugged it in. I shook my mouse, and the screen glowed to life.

I sat down, determined to get answers. And, after my research, if I discovered that there was something going on in Harmony Island, I was going to expose it. This Sunday, in the paper.

I just hoped my relationship with Asher could withstand that kind of blow. No matter how I pitched it, Asher was embroiled in a scandal, and there was no way I could save him.

I could keep this under wraps, but that wasn't who I was. The residents of Harmony Island deserved to know, so I was going to tell them.

19

JUNIPER

SWEET TEA & SOUTHERN GENTLEMAN

Time always seemed to stand still when I was waiting for something. I was standing at the register the next day, willing the seconds to tick by faster, ready to get my lunch with Kevin over. I was ready to put him firmly in my rearview mirror so I could finally start living.

I was finally ready to be Mrs. Kevin Proctor no more.

I tapped my fingers next to the register as I mentally fought the urge to pull out my phone from the drawer. I was trying to keep myself from glancing at the screen just to see how many minutes *hadn't* passed by. I blew out my breath and glanced around, needing a distraction.

I had exactly fifteen minutes until I needed to leave. And with the way I was feeling, they were going to be the longest fifteen minutes of my life.

Of course, the store was slow. The last customer had

come through my register twenty minutes ago, and not a single person had walked in since then.

Boone had kept to himself since last night. This morning, he'd been up early. By the time I came out, he was showered and had made breakfast—French toast with bacon. We ate in silence at the dinner table, and then he waited for me while I grabbed my shoes. We left the house walking side by side, me to my car and him to his truck.

When we got to the store, we parted ways, and he'd kept to the back most of the morning. I tipped my gaze up toward the ceiling. What I wouldn't give for someone to come in and engage me in conversation. I'd even take a call from my mother at this point.

But I doubted she would oblige. They'd been so busy in California that all I'd gotten was random texts here and there. Some were to remind me of a delivery to the store. The others must have been butt-dials because they made no sense.

I was glad my parents were enjoying themselves, and I was grateful they'd been gone long enough for me to figure out what I wanted to do with Kevin. By the time Mom and Dad were back, my divorce would be well on its way, and I would be ready to start my new life as a single mom.

My hand pressed my stomach at that thought. *Single mom.*

Of all the ways I'd seen my life going, this possibility was not even a blip on my radar. Now, I had to think about that baby first and foremost. I had been bumped to second string.

"Hey, when were you wanting to take lunch?"

Boone's voice startled me. I yelped and turned to see him standing right behind me with his eyebrows raised as if he hadn't anticipated my reaction.

I swallowed, my mouth running dry as all thought left my mind. "I, um...er." *Speak, woman!* I cleared my throat and grounded myself. "I can go now," I finally managed out.

Boone looked confused, but I just stepped out of the register alcove and waved for him to enter. He glanced over at me but obeyed.

"I was getting nauseous from hunger, anyway," I said as I shot him a big smile.

He nodded. "Okay."

"Awesome," I said as I snapped my fingers. "I'm just going to eat some food I have in the back." I pinched my lips shut. I wanted to give Boone a reason why I wouldn't be going through the checkout with my food. But my words just came out squeaky and desperate.

If I didn't get out of here, I was going to find myself confessing that I was meeting Kevin at the diner without Boone even speaking a single word.

"I'm going to go," I said, turning on my heel and hurrying away.

By the time I got to the back room, my heart was racing. Nerves from seeing Kevin mixed with lying to Boone came crashing together into a vortex, and I was shaking. I was sweating and shivering at the same time.

Maybe this was a strange pregnancy symptom. I entertained that thought for a moment before I shook my head. No. This was definitely a symptom of everything going on externally with me right now. I couldn't blame the baby for this one.

I grabbed my purse from Mom's office, pulled the strap up onto my shoulder, and headed out the back door. I was going to walk to the diner today. The fresh air and sunshine were going to help me prepare my mind for seeing Kevin and for what I was going to say.

The walk was uneventful. I waved to a few Harmony residents, and thankfully, they didn't stop to talk to me. They seemed to be just as distracted as I was.

By the time I got to Harmony Island Diner, I was warm but not quite sweaty, which I was grateful for. I didn't want to show up to see Kevin sweating like a stuck pig. I walked past the sign, but something caused me to pause. Where it used to say Harmony Island Diner, it now said Sunny Side-Up Diner. The sign was painted with bright oranges and blues, and it was adorable.

I pulled open the door and walked into the restaurant. The sign, *Please Wait to be Seated*, greeted me at the hostess stand. I paused and glanced around. I knew from the parking lot that Kevin wasn't here yet, which filled me relief. I'd wanted to get here first so I could pick the table. Nothing worse than walking into a tricky situation without an escape plan.

Thankfully, I only had to wait a minute before a woman pushed through the kitchen doors. Her hair was pulled up into a messy bun with wisps framing her face. Her gaze met mine and she quickly set down the tray of utensils she was carrying and hurried over to me, wiping her hands on her apron as she approached.

"I'm so sorry," she said as she shot me an apologetic smile. "Were you waiting long?" She was at the hostess stand now, reaching down to grab a menu. I read her name tag, *Willow*.

I shook my head. "No. Not long." She straightened, but I raised my hand. "There'll be two of us."

She nodded, reaching down to grab another menu. "Come with me," she said as she turned and walked me through the restaurant.

We got to the far table, and she glanced over at me as if to ask if this was okay. I nodded, and she started laying the menus down as I took a seat. She asked me if she could get me something to drink, and I ordered waters for me and Kevin. I knew he would probably want something more, but I'd let him order that when he got here.

Willow dropped off the waters, and I spent what felt like an eternity sipping it and constantly glancing toward the front door. Kevin was officially ten minutes late, which wasn't like him. I reached into my purse to pull out my phone and came up empty-handed.

I dumped the contents of my purse out onto the table in front of me as my stomach sank. Crap. I'd left it in the drawer at the register. Of course, I did. I'd been so distracted by Boone that I'd forgotten to grab it.

If Kevin had canceled on me, I wasn't going to get the message.

My stomach growled as I glanced around. Five minutes later, Willow approached me with a cautious smile. She asked if I wanted to just go ahead and order. My first instinct was to say no, but I was hungry and my ice water was no longer keeping those pains at bay. So, I ordered chicken strips and French fries. She nodded as she tucked her pad into her apron and slipped her pen behind her ear. She told me she'd put that right in before she left to help an older couple who'd just come in.

They had to be in their seventies. He was holding her hand as they waited for Willow to grab their menus and lead them to their seats. I couldn't help but watch as they shuffled to their table. He pulled out her chair for her to sit. She smiled up at him after she was settled. He made his way to his seat, and then they turned their attention to Willow.

There was a time in my life when I'd wanted the same for me. When I thought that was going to be Kevin and I. But that dream was buried six feet under and there was no way I was going to dig it up. I was here to put my marriage to rest, and I was excited and nervous for the prospects of the unknown. I was ready to walk into the future, alone.

If only Kevin would get here so I could actually say those words out loud.

Willow delivered my chicken strips and French fries, and I was halfway through the plate when the chair next to me was suddenly pulled out. I startled, expecting to see Kevin standing there, but instead I was met with the man who had pulled out of my parents' driveway yesterday morning.

I stared at him, confused why he was in the process of sitting next to me. "Excuse me. I am waiting for someone."

The man didn't look phased as he stared at me. "I know. Mr. Proctor sent me. Name's Collin Baker."

Confusion swirled in my mind. Did he just say Mr. Proctor? "I think you have the wrong person," I said.

He shook his head. "No, I don't. You're Juniper Proctor, and your husband, Kevin, sent me."

I stared at him. "H-how do you know my husband?"

The man extended his hand as if he expected me to take it. "I work for his father, Mr. Marcus Proctor."

When it became apparent that I wasn't going to shake his hand, he dropped it into his lap and leaned against the chair. I could tell that this was not his normal day-to-day job. He was doing this as a favor for the family.

"Why were you in my driveway yesterday morning?" I asked. My brain was scrambling to put together the pieces, and I was coming up short every time. What was I missing?

"I was on official business yesterday morning. It's

nothing I can discuss with you." He folded his arms across his chest.

"Well, why are you here instead of Kevin?" I asked. In all honesty, I just wanted him to leave. The food I just consumed now sat like a rock in my stomach. And the last thing I wanted was to lose my lunch just moments after eating it. But if he lingered, that was going to become a very real reality.

"Kevin asked me to come to tell you he's not able to make it today. He said you weren't answering his texts. He didn't want to leave you here alone, so he asked me if I could run by and tell you."

"Oh." That was all I could say. I came to the diner with such hope for closure and the ability to move on. But it seemed like I wasn't going to get any of those things. My future was once again stagnant. And I hated it. "Well, thanks for coming to tell me."

He nodded, looking as if he had done his job, as he stood and pushed his chair back under the table. He said a quick goodbye and headed back towards the front door, not pausing to wait for me to return the sentiment.

I wasn't sure how long I sat there trying to process what had just happened, but when Willow came over and asked me if I was finished with my plate, I realized I had sat here for quite a while. If I didn't get back to the store, Boone was going to send a search party for me.

And that's when reality hit me, and it hit me hard. If this

man worked for Marcus Proctor, and he was talking to Boon yesterday in the wee hours of the morning. Did that mean...

I wanted to throw up, cry, and scream all at the same time. My brain had put together the pieces of the puzzle, and yet I was unwilling to stare at the final product. The final product that had my heart ripping to pieces.

Boone worked for the Proctors.

The man who I'd stupidly thought, in some sort of mystical, kismet way, was sent to my family to protect me, was not fate finally showering me with good fortune. No, he was just another proof of the manipulation of the Proctor family. He was the doorway back into my life that Kevin needed. And I was the stupid prey who'd let him in.

Tears brimmed my eyes. I felt stupid and ridiculous and naïve all at the same time. I'd let myself get close to this man. I'd let him into my home. I'd told him my secrets.

Oh God.

The baby.

Had he told Kevin about the baby? What about the Proctors? I doubted that Marcus or Candice were going to let me raise this child all on my own. If they knew that I was pregnant, they would be speaking to a lawyer. The baby would to be taken from me the moment it was born.

Fear crashed into me. Willow approached the table, but I wasn't in the mood to speak so I grabbed a twenty out of my wallet and slammed it down on the table. Before she could ask me if I wanted the change, I pushed out my chair and hurried to the front door. Thankfully, she didn't follow after me.

It wasn't until I was out on the sidewalk that hot tears started flowing down my cheeks. Luckily, I knew the way back to the grocery store like the back of my hand, so I didn't really need to see where I was going. I tried to muffle the sobs that wanted to escape. I didn't want to cry over Boone. I wanted to be stronger than this. But I was heartbroken.

By the time I got to the store, and was standing outside, staring up at the sign, I realized walking back into this place was the last thing I wanted to do. I didn't want to face Boone. I didn't want to face the reality of what the future was going to hold. I'd been so optimistic about things when I woke up this morning, and now it had crumbled before me faster than I could blink.

I wanted to go home.

I fished my keys from my purse and walked to the back of the store where I'd parked my car. I opened the door and climbed inside. I found a napkin in the center console and wiped my tears. I started the engine and pulled out of my parking spot.

A sense of relief washed over me as I drove up my parents' driveway and turned off the engine. I couldn't wait to get into my room, where I would shut the door—shut out reality. There I could think about what I was going to do. How I was going to handle all of this.

I'd expected Kevin to betray me. That's what he always did.

I just never thought Boone would do the same.

Just as I pushed through the front door and into my parents' house, a familiar sound stopped me. My mother's voice.

They were back?

A sob escaped my lips as the tears began to flow once more. I hurriedly shut the door and rushed to the kitchen, where her voice was coming from. But no one was there.

I was alone.

I stared at the machine, realizing that my mom had called to leave herself a message. Something about not forgetting to set up a doctor's appointment for my dad when they got back. Also, she reminded herself that she needed to check on Mrs. Boulder.

The sound of my mom's voice mixed with the pain in my chest, and I found myself acting before I could think. I needed to talk to my mom. I needed to hear her tell me everything was going to be okay. So, I reached forward, grabbed the phone and pressed the talk button.

She was in the middle of leaving her message when the dam broke inside of me. Tears were flowing now, and my voice crackled as I sobbed out, "Mom."

20

BOONE

SWEET TEA & SOUTHERN GENTLEMAN

Juniper wasn't back yet.

I stood at the register, staring at an elderly woman unloading her groceries onto the conveyor belt. I knew she wasn't actually moving at a snail's pace. My frustration had nothing to do with her and everything to do with the fact that Juniper had made plans to meet Kevin and didn't tell me.

I'd only found out from the texts that were currently blowing up her phone. I'd tried to ignore the buzzing coming from the drawer under the register. I'd figured that Juniper had unknowingly left her phone behind. But when the noise became constant and incessant, I pulled the drawer open only to find that the sender was Kevin, and—from what I could see in the message preview on her lock screen—he wasn't coming to lunch.

I was now in the midst of trying to figure out when she

made these plans and why she didn't tell me. I thought we'd gotten closer. I thought she trusted me. And even though she had no obligation to tell me where she was going, I'd deluded myself into thinking that she would.

I thought I meant enough to her to at least deserve that.

Apparently, I was wrong.

The conveyor brought the woman's groceries to me, so I started scanning them. I wanted to force thoughts of Juniper to the far corners of my mind, where I shoved a lot of things, but no matter how much I tried *not* to think about her, it wasn't working.

She was all I could think about.

I don't know if it was my anxiety about Juniper or my growing ability to run the register, but I finished scanning the woman's items, bagged them, and walked around the register to load them into her cart in record time.

I loaded her groceries while she used the pin pad to pay. The register clocked the payment and spit out the receipt, which I tore off and handed to her. She took it and thanked me before she pushed her cart through the sliding doors.

Now alone, I stared at the register as I tried to ignore the newest text message that had just come through. Kevin was nothing if not persistent.

And where the hell was Juniper? She'd left forty minutes ago. Actually, she'd told me she was going to go eat lunch forty minutes ago. I had no idea when she actually left the store.

My stomach twisted at that thought. How was I supposed to protect her if she didn't tell me things? And why did she feel like she needed to lie? I wasn't here to stop her—I wasn't going to do that. But I would make sure she was safe. She had to know that.

Or maybe I just misread everything that had transpired between us over the last week. Maybe I was the only one who hoped our time together meant something more. And Juniper was just trying to figure out how she was going to get back with Kevin.

I was going to be the idiot left holding my heart after she tore it from my chest.

I cursed as I pushed my hand through my hair and tipped my face toward the ceiling. If that was true, then why did I want to grab my keys, get into my truck, and drive to find her just to make sure she was okay?

Even if I found her in the arms of Kevin—I needed to make sure she was safe.

I was an idiot.

I grabbed my key and locked the register. I slipped Juniper's phone into my back pocket as I headed toward the bakery. I wasn't going to be able to concentrate until I knew Juniper was safe. Even if it meant breaking my heart, I was going to find her.

Kate was behind the bakery counter, wiping down a mixer. I tapped on the metal counter, which drew her attention over.

"Hey, Boone," she said as she set the rag down and

headed over to me. "You okay?" she asked as she got closer and raked her gaze over my face.

"Juniper left for lunch, but I'm not sure if she got there. Her"— I swallowed at the acid that rose up in my throat when I thought about Kevin—"lunch date keeps texting her. And she left her phone at the register." I pulled her phone from my back pocket and held it up for Kate to see.

Kate's eyes widened as she nodded and started pulling her apron strings. "Of course. Yes, I can help," she said as she slipped her apron over her head and set it down on the counter. "Go find Juniper."

I left the register key with her and headed to the back room. I was grateful that Kate knew what to do and I wasn't going to waste time walking her through how to run a register. I pushed through the back doors and over to my locker to grab my truck keys. I slammed the door shut and didn't stop until I had yanked open my driver's door and climbed inside. Juniper's car was gone, which meant she'd driven. I was thankful for that. All I needed to do now was find her car and then I'd find her.

I didn't know where to start looking, so I drove slowly around the neighboring buildings. When I came up empty-handed, I went further out. When I passed by Harmony Island Diner—now Sunny Side-Up Diner—I paused. Last time she went out with Kevin, it had been there. Maybe Kevin was a man of habit.

I flipped on my blinker and turned right into the parking lot. I found the nearest parking spot and pulled into it. I grabbed my keys from the ignition and climbed out of my truck.

The diner was quiet when I pulled open the door. The woman who ran this place was in the process of cleaning a table when I rounded the hostess stand in search of someone to talk to.

"Table for one?" she asked when her gaze met mine.

"I'm not here to eat."

Her lips formed a "o" shape.

"I'm looking for Juniper Godwin..." I flicked my gaze down to her name tag. "Willow," I added.

She nodded. "She left about fifteen minutes ago. Some guy came to meet her, and after he left she was in tears. Didn't really want to talk to me and left." She waved to the plate of half-eaten chicken strips and fries. "This is all that's left of her lunch."

I paused as I glanced toward the door and then back to Willow. "Did she tell you where she was going?"

Willow shook her head. "No. She just left in a hurry."

I nodded, grateful that she'd at least gotten here safely. Now to figure out where she went. I thanked Willow and headed back out to the parking lot. Once I was in my truck, I threw it in reverse and pulled out of the parking spot. When I got to the road, I glanced left and then right before making the choice to turn right.

I'd drive through town quick, and if I didn't see her car, I'd head to the Godwin's house. I doubted she'd go home, so that was going to be the last place I checked.

Thirty minutes later I was cursing myself for not having to gone to the Godwin's house first. Every place I drove, I came up empty, so I headed out of town to the Godwin's place. Of course, her car parked in the driveway was the first thing I saw when I turned down their street.

Relief flooded my body as I pulled up alongside her car and turned off the engine. She was here and she was safe.

I was out of my truck and across the yard in record time. I'm sure I looked strange to all the neighbors with how fast I was moving. I pulled open the front door and kicked off my shoes before shutting the door behind me.

"Juniper?" I called out when I didn't see her in the living room or the kitchen.

No answer.

I made my way down the hallway, glancing in all the rooms with open doors. She wasn't in any of them. When I got to her room, I knocked on the door and waited. She had to be in here. Unless...

Unless Kevin picked her up and she really wasn't home.

I closed my eyes, cursing myself for being so stupid. Just as I turned to leave, Juniper's door opened, and suddenly, I was staring into Juniper's bloodshot eyes. My gaze drifted down to her tear-stained cheeks and her downturned lips.

"What happened?" I asked, my voice coming out deeper than I'd intended. "Did he hurt you?" I was over this man. I was finished sitting on the sidelines while he hurt Juniper.

"What are you doing here?" she asked, fire burning in her gaze in a way I'd never seen before.

I frowned. "You didn't come back to the store. I was worried about you." I stepped closer to her as the desire to wrap my arms around her and pull her close washed through me. She was safe, and that was all I cared about.

"You shouldn't have come." She stepped back as if we were two magnets repelling each other.

"You left your phone." I pulled it out of my back pocket and offered it to her.

She looked at it for a moment before she held out her hand and let me drop her phone into her palm. "I need you to leave." She wrapped her fingers around the phone.

I stared at her, confused by her reaction. "Are you okay?" I asked. "Did Kevin—"

"I'm not going to talk to you about Kevin." She wrapped her arms around her chest as if she were hugging herself.

"Okay," I said. I'd never tried to push her out of her comfort zone. If she wanted to keep to herself, I was more than willing to let her do that.

"You should be ashamed of yourself." Juniper's words were cold and sliced through me like a hot knife through butter. I stared at her as I tried to figure out what she was saying. "How could you do that? Make me trust you when it was all a lie." Her eyes narrowed.

"Juniper, I..." Did she find out about my mom? Did she learn about how I'd failed her? Did she realize it was a sad joke that I thought I could somehow make up for my failure by saving her?

"How long were you going to keep pretending? Was it until I told you all my secrets?"

Tears flooded her eyes, and that's when I realized why she was crying. It wasn't because of Kevin. It was because of...me.

"You made me trust you. I told you things I wouldn't tell anyone else." Her voice was cracking, and with each tear that slid down her cheek, my heart shattered again and again. "Get out of my house."

I stared at her. I didn't want to leave. She made me feel alive. She was my sun, my moon, the air I needed to breathe. I feared that if I left, I'd die.

I didn't want to leave, but my presence was breaking her. I wanted to fix this; I just didn't know how.

"I wish you'd never come here," she whispered. "I can't believe I listened to your lies."

"I'm so sorry, Juniper." That was all I could say. I wanted to change her mind about me, but anything I said would be a lie. She was right for walking away. For asking me to leave. I didn't deserve to be around her. I'd been selfish for too long. And if I didn't obey her request and leave, I was never going to have the strength to walk away.

"Yeah right." Her gaze was dark as she glared at me. "Just tell Kevin that we're over."

I frowned. Tell Kevin? Why would I tell Kevin?

But before I could get the question out, she stepped back and closed the door behind her, leaving me to stare at the dark wood. I wanted to knock on the door. I wanted to ask her what she meant. But I realized that was an exercise in futility. She wanted me gone, so I was going to leave.

The last thing I wanted to do was hurt her, and standing in her hallway seemed to be breaking her in a way that I could never forgive myself for. So, I was going to walk away.

I headed into the living room and shoved my things into my bag. I grabbed my toothbrush and toothpaste from the bathroom and walked back into the living room. I passed by my bag and grabbed the strap as I swung it up onto my shoulder.

I pulled open the front door and locked it before I shut it behind me. I bounded down the front steps and over to my truck. I threw my bag into the bed and climbed into the driver's seat. I threw it into reverse and backed out of the driveway.

I wasn't sure where I was going. I thought about going back to the shop. After all, I'd kind of left Kate there to fend for herself. But the last thing I wanted was for Juniper to show up and see me there. It was apparent that I'd already put her through hell, I wasn't going to do it again.

I drove around town for about an hour before I found myself parked outside of Harmony Cove. I stared at the houses that lined the main road leading into the community. This was the only place on the island where I actually belonged. And that was a stretch.

I took a right and drove until I found myself parked in front of Mom's house. It looked exactly like it had yesterday morning. I turned off my engine and threw my keys onto the passenger seat before reclining all the way back. I stared up at the ceiling of my truck and took in a deep breath.

I closed my eyes as my conversation with Juniper played in a loop in my mind. I shook my head as my entire body ached to go back to her. To pull her close and protect her forever. She was hurting, and I would do anything to take that hurt away.

The problem was, I was the one who had hurt her. I would never, ever forgive myself for that. She deserved the world. So, I was going to leave her alone. And when everything was settled with my mother's house, I'd leave Harmony for good.

I'd fallen in love with Juniper, but she didn't feel the same. I didn't blame her. After what I'd done, she was right to walk away. I just hoped she'd find the happiness she deserved. I'd wanted to give her that happiness—but it was clear now, I'd never get the chance.

I was already dead, but she has so much life left. It was time I got out of her way and let her live it.

21

JUNIPER

SWEET TEA &
SOUTHERN GENTLEMAN

My entire body ached as I rolled over and grabbed my phone from my nightstand Friday morning. My eyes hurt. My throat hurt. My body hurt.

I'd spent the night tossing and turning, unable to get Boone's stare out of my head. He looked so broken and confused as he stood in my hallway after I told him to leave. Once I shut the door, I spent an eternity battling with myself until the desire to pull open the door and retract my words won. But he was gone by then. Everything that he owned was gone.

He was nothing but a memory etched into my mind.

I was strong enough to fight the urge to get in my car and drive after him. Instead, I spent the night eating ice cream and binge watching 90's sitcoms on TV. I'd fallen asleep on the couch only to wake up at 2 a.m. with a sugar headache and a crick in my neck.

I forced myself up, brushed my teeth, crawled into bed, and slept until...

Nine?

I pulled my covers off my body and rolled out of bed. I was going to be late opening the store. I stumbled into my bathroom and started the shower. Once I was clean, I dressed and headed out to the kitchen to make myself some food. Nausea had a way of hitting me like a semi-truck if I didn't eat religiously.

Just as I rounded the wall and headed into the kitchen, a familiar sight caused me to stop. Mom was standing at the oven and Dad was sitting at the table with the newspaper opened in front of him.

I blinked before rubbing my eyes and glancing around at them once more. "Mom?"

Mom turned, and suddenly the spatula was dropping from her hand and she was crossing the space between us. Her arms wrapped me up into one of her rib-crushing hugs.

"Juniper, I'm so glad you're okay," she whispered, tears brimming her eyes as her voice cracked from emotion.

"You came back," I said, tears brimming my eyes as well. This was exactly what I needed. But then guilt washed over me. "What about Aunt Christi?"

Mom waved away my comment. "She told us we had to go. She's in good hands with her doctor, and I told her once things were settled here, we'd be back." She held my gaze. "You need me here."

The tears that I'd tried so hard to keep at bay started

flowing. Mom was right. I did need her. I needed her here with me, or I wasn't going to get though the day.

Mom started crying as well. But instead of taking care of herself, she wiped my tears, took my hand, and sat me down at the table.

I was too tired and exhausted to fight her. Dad was watching us. I could tell that he wanted to jump in, but he didn't know what to say. So he just sat there. I smiled at him to let him know that I appreciated his presence.

Mom sat on the chair next to mine. She brushed her tears from her cheeks and focused on me.

My stomach growled, and I felt a wave of nausea come over me. There was no way I was going to make it through what I needed to say to her without some food, so I reached across the table and rested my hand on hers.

"Can I eat first?"

Mom sprang to life. She nodded as she stood and headed back over to the stove, where she had been making some pancakes. I sat, enjoying the familiarity of my parents in the kitchen. I needed this more than I'd realized.

Ten minutes later, Mom placed a plate in front of me and another in front of Dad. She poured me a glass of milk and got Dad a fresh cup of coffee. When she returned to the table with her own plate, I was in the midst of eating. But I knew if I didn't say what I needed to say to them, I was going to lose my courage.

"I'm pregnant," I whispered as I stared at the half-eaten pancakes in front of me.

Mom gasped, but Dad was quiet. I waited for them to say something, but there was no other response. I finally gathered my courage and looked up to see my parents staring at me.

"It's Kevin's. I just found out last week. I don't want to be married to him anymore. He doesn't know about the baby, and I'm too scared to tell him. I don't want him or the Proctors to take the baby away from me, but I feel powerless to stop them." The words tumbled from my lips. Every worry that I'd had over the last week left my mouth and hung in the air like a dark cloud on a rainy day.

Were Mom and Dad disappointed in me? I was married, and if I were in a normal, healthy marriage, a pregnancy would be welcomed. But because I was with Kevin, this baby wasn't the wonderful surprise that it should be.

"Oh, Juniper." Mom was out of her chair and came over to me. She wrapped her arms around me and pulled me close. "I'm going to be a nana," she whispered.

I sat there, a little stunned by her reaction. I heard the sound of Dad's chair legs scraping the floor, and a moment later, his arms were wrapped around Mom and me. "A baby is a wonderful blessing," he murmured.

Relief washed through me. My parents were excited for me. They were excited for the baby. It was like I'd been in a deep sleep and I was finally able to wake up. With Mom and Dad behind me, I could do anything.

I wrapped my arms around them, and we just held each other. The past. Our history. It was healing in a way that I'd never thought possible. They'd wanted nothing more than for me to come home, and I wanted nothing more than to stay here until I healed.

Dad was the first to break the hug. Mom was sniffling as she pulled back. She placed her hands on either side of my face and held my gaze. "The Proctors will have another thing coming if they think they can swoop in here and take this baby. Your dad and I will fight alongside you and protect you, understand? You don't need to be scared."

I nodded, tears flowing down my cheeks. I heard Dad humph in agreement. "Thanks," was all I could manage out.

Mom returned to her seat. "Now, tell me what happened with Boone."

My heart squeezed at the sound of his name. Pain coursed through me as I studied Mom. Of course, she was going to want to know about what happened. But I didn't want to talk about it. It hurt too much to even think about him.

But they were going to push until I told them, and I was tired of keeping secrets. Perhaps telling them what happened between Boone and me would help me feel better. It was at least worth a shot.

So I told them about Collin Baker. I told them about how he was having meetings with Boone. I told them how Collin showed up for lunch instead of Kevin, and I told them how Boone never denied any of the accusations I threw at him last night. And instead of staying and explaining himself, he'd just left.

The one thing I did leave out was the fact that I was certain I'd fallen for him. That even though he'd betrayed me, I still cared about him. He took care of me when I needed him the most, and that was something I was never going to forget.

I was never going to forget him, no matter how hard I tried.

Mom and Dad were surprised—especially Dad. They didn't really say much, just that they were disappointed that Boone had fooled us all.

"He did do something helpful before he left," I said as I pushed some crumbs around on the tabletop.

"He did?" Mom asked.

I nodded. "He set me up an appointment with a lawyer today." I glanced at Mom and then Dad. "I'm divorcing Kevin."

Mom glanced over at Dad, who nodded. "I'll come with you," Mom said as she turned back to meet my gaze.

"I'm okay," I whispered.

Mom shook her head. "No, I'm going with you."

"I'll go to the store, and you go with your mother." Dad was standing now, his gaze dark and his expression sharp. He narrowed his eyes at me, and I could feel his anger and hatred for Kevin as he said, "You go there and you do everything to make sure that son of a bitch gets nothing."

I nodded before Dad turned and headed out of the dining room.

After I helped Mom clean up after breakfast, we spent

some time looking at baby clothes online. For the first time since finding out about the baby, I felt excited. But when I climbed into Mom's car at eleven to make our way to the lawyer's office, a sense of dread washed over me.

I was on my way to divorce this baby's father. Even though I knew that I was doing the right thing, I still felt guilty. I loved this baby more than anything, and if I could give it the world, I would.

I was scared of my future as a single mom, but it was better this way.

We walked out of the lawyer's office an hour later, feeling better. Mr. Phillips was supportive and he was confident that this would be an easy process. Even though it would require me speaking about the abuse I suffered with Kevin, he was certain that the judge wouldn't let Kevin railroad me like I'd feared.

Mom held the door for me as we called a goodbye and stepped out onto the sidewalk. Mom wrapped her arm around my shoulder, and we made our way to her car in the parking lot.

"How are you feeling?" she asked.

I glanced over at her, but just as I did, I caught sight of a black truck. I paused, my heart picking up speed as I watched it turn right and disappear down the road. The truck looked like Boone's, but then I shook my head. That wasn't Boone. I was ridiculous to think that it was.

Boone was probably long gone by now. He wasn't hanging around Harmony.

"Better," I finally said, turning to focus on Mom, who was studying me. I smiled. "Hungry."

She laughed as she dropped her arm and made her way to the driver's door. I followed suit, making my way toward the passenger door.

We were both in the car with the doors shut and our seatbelts on when my phone chimed. Mom put the car in reverse and backed out of the parking spot as I fished around in my purse for my phone. For a second, I allowed myself to think that it was a message from Boone, but when I saw Kevin's name, my heart sank.

He knew.

"Who is it?" Mom asked as she pulled out onto Main Street.

I'd made myself a promise to tell my parents the truth, so I whispered, "It's Kevin."

Mom was quiet for a moment before she asked, "What does he want?"

I punched in my passcode, and his text flashed on my screen.

Kevin: I'm so sorry for yesterday. I had a meeting I couldn't get out of. Can we meet for dinner tonight? I really need to talk to you.

And then, a moment later, another text came through.

Kevin: Please?

My fingers hovered over the keyboard. Mom kept glancing at me, and I could feel her question in her gaze.

"Mom, I need to talk to him," I said. I knew that wasn't

what she wanted to hear, but it was the truth. I glanced over at her. "He deserves to hear about the baby, and I can't tell him over text."

"Juniper, no. That's not a good idea."

Mom's voice had turned desperate now, but I was going to stand my ground on this. "I'll be fine," I said as I turned my attention outside.

"Juniper."

"Mom!" As quickly as my voice rose, I brought it back down as I turned to her. "Please, I need to do this." I held her gaze as she lingered at a red light. "I will be fine." I needed her to know that I had to do this. If I didn't, I would never be able to fully move on.

I needed to prove to myself that I was stronger than Kevin had led me to believe. I was ready to take my strength back. Besides, the broken heart that Boone gave me hurt worse than anything Kevin could do to me. I needed to stare Kevin in the face and tell him that we were over. That I was moving on without him.

He could have Boone. I was done.

Mom narrowed her eyes, but I just held her gaze with all the strength I could muster. "I'm going, Mom," I said as I folded my arms across my chest and stared out the windshield. "And there's nothing you can say that will stop me."

22

BOONE

The afternoon sun beat down on me as I sat in the driver's seat of my truck. I was mindlessly scrolling though a social media app on my phone as I tried hard *not* to think about Juniper. I'd made the stupid decision to drive by the lawyer's office earlier to see if she was there, only to see her standing on the sidewalk with her mom.

I prayed that she didn't see me as I took the first available right and drove down some residential streets until I was certain she couldn't find me if she wanted to.

I'd been worried that she was doing this alone, so when I saw Mrs. Godwin I felt both relieved and worried. They were home, which meant Juniper had told them I'd disappointed her. I couldn't only imagine what they thought of me now.

I sighed as I closed my eyes and tipped my head back. I'd slept in my truck last night, and my body ached. I didn't want to admit it, but I knew my broken heart was the cause of most of that pain.

I missed Juniper and worried about her at the same time. It was a circle of hell that I never knew existed. But I'd stay here if it meant Juniper was happy.

A soft knock on my car door had me sitting up and glancing over. I half expected to see one of the neighbors coming over to see if I were alive. Instead, I was staring into the eyes of Mrs. Godwin. Her eyebrows were drawn together as she studied me.

"Mrs. Godwin?" I asked as I sat up straighter before peeking over at her once more.

"Boone." Then she frowned. "What are you doing here?" she asked as she glanced around.

I hurriedly opened my door. Thankfully, she must have anticipated what I was going to do, because she stepped out of the way. I jumped to the ground and slammed the door behind me. I pushed my hand through my hair and glanced over at her once more.

"This is my mom's house," I whispered, hating that she was standing here, staring at me. I felt raw. Like my entire history had been exposed in an instant.

She ran her gaze over the house before she turned back to me. "Oh," she said softly.

I frowned as what was happening finally caught up with me. "What are you doing here?" Then I paused. "How did you know where to find me?"

Mrs. Godwin waved away my comment. "Honey, this is

a small town. Secrets don't stay secret for very long." My look must have told her that I didn't believe her. A moment later, she sighed. "I was at the post office, and I overheard Ewin asking Patty if someone had bought Hannah Grimes' house down the street. He said that there was a black truck parked in the driveway overnight." She waved to my truck. "I knew it had to be you."

"Oh." I shoved my hands into my front pockets and shrugged. I should have known my presence would draw the attention of the residents in Harmony Cove.

We stood in silence for a few moments before she turned her attention back to me. "What happened, Boone?"

I closed my eyes as I fought the emotions that rose up in my chest. I didn't know how much truth to tell her. I didn't want yet another person to look at me like Juniper had last night.

When I didn't respond right away, she took in a deep breath. "How do you know Collin Baker?"

I looked at her. "Collin Baker?"

She nodded.

"He's been calling me about acquiring my mom's house." I nodded toward the house. Mrs. Godwin followed my gesture. "I've been trying to ignore his phone calls. He came to your house Wednesday morning, but I told him to go away." I blew out my breath. "I'm not ready to sell."

Mrs. Godwin narrowed her eyes. "I need you to answer every one of my questions." She held up her forefinger. "No lies."

I nodded. "Of course."

"Are you working for Kevin?"

Her question startled me. My eyes widened. Is that what Juniper thought? "Of course not."

Mrs. Godwin studied me before she nodded. "Did you tell Collin or Kevin about the baby?"

A wave of protective energy surged in my chest. "Hell no."

Mrs. Godwin didn't seem phased by my response. "Good." Then she grew serious once more. "Did you share any personal information about Juniper?"

I shook my head. "I don't know Kevin or Collin. I've only talked to Collin about my mom's house, and if I saw Kevin again..." My voice trailed off. I didn't want to expose Mrs. Godwin to the slew of curse words that were about to leave my mouth.

I refocused my thoughts as I held Mrs. Godwin's gaze. "I would do anything to protect Juniper and that baby." My voice broke, but I continued anyway. "I would give my life just so they could live." That was easy. They deserved to be happy. I didn't.

Mrs. Godwin's eyes widened at my confession. And then a knowing look passed through her gaze. "You love my daughter?" she asked.

It was the first time I'd heard those words spoken out loud. I stood there, processing what she'd just asked me, but also knowing that I swore to tell the truth. So I just nodded. "I do."

She was silent for a moment. "Good. Then you'll help me."

I frowned. "Help you with what?"

She sighed as she pinched the bridge of her nose. "She's meeting Kevin tonight."

I swore.

"I told her not to go. I told her to ignore him. But she wants to say goodbye. She thinks she owes it to him."

"Juniper," I whispered under my breath.

"I need you to be there. You don't have to let her know that you're there, but I need someone to protect her." She narrowed her eyes. "Can you do that?"

"Of course."

She held my gaze before she nodded. "Good. I'll find out where they are meeting, and I will text you."

"Okay."

She paused before she suddenly wrapped her arms around me and pulled me into a hug. She held me for a moment before letting go. Her eyes were brimming with tears as she studied me. "You're a good man, Boone." She glanced over to my mother's house and then back to me. "Your mom would have been proud of the son she raised." She smiled at me. "I know I would be."

My heart ached at her words. I wanted to tell her to stop talking, but at the same time, I didn't want her to stop. I didn't deserve her praise. If only she knew how I'd failed the one person I should have protected. "Thanks," was all I could whisper.

Mrs. Godwin lifted her hand and rested it on my cheek as she smiled up at me. "Whatever happened between the two of you, I'm sure she just wants the best for you." She shrugged. "That's all moms want."

The emotions in my throat felt like they were strangling me. I knew I wasn't going to be able to speak, so I just nodded.

She patted my cheek a few times before she pulled back and smiled at me once more. "I'll text you," she said before she fished around in her purse for her keys and pulled them out.

I nodded again.

She said goodbye, and thankfully, I managed out a goodbye as well. She smiled as she made her way over to her car and climbed inside. I waved at her as she drove down the road. I lingered outside my truck until her car was out of sight.

Now alone, I pulled open the door and climbed inside. My body felt like dead weight as I sat in the seat and stared out the windshield. I was grateful that Mrs. Godwin came. At least now, Juniper's reaction yesterday made sense. I'd felt so confused with her standing there looking so hurt and broken.

I wanted to rush to her. I wanted to explain what had happened. But I feared the trust between us was already broken. Would she open herself up to me again?

Did I deserve that?

I stared at Mom's house. I knew the truth before I could

even think the words. Juniper deserved someone better than me. I was too broken for her. If I truly loved her like I told Mrs. Godwin I did, then I would walk away. I would let her find someone who could give her more than I could. I didn't want her to have to carry my baggage.

She was pure and perfect, and I was a beast.

I shook my head. Once I made sure she was safe, I was going to leave and never look back.

If I confessed everything to her and she asked me to stay, I would never be able to leave. Even though I knew leaving was better for her. Keeping my distance was the only way I was going to survive.

I not only needed to keep her safe from Kevin, I needed to keep her safe from me. I'd fulfill my promise, and then I would leave. Even if it broke me, I would leave.

I had to.

23

JUNIPER

SWEET TEA & SOUTHERN GENTLEMAN

I didn't expect Kevin's rental house to be as big as it was. The front door was massive with a giant ornate window in the middle of it. I felt dwarfed as I stood next to it. My confidence waned as I raised my hand and knocked a few times on the solid oak.

Thoughts of my conversation with Mom floated through my mind before I forced them out. Mom didn't want me to come. She feared what Kevin would do to me. Of course, there was always a chance things would go south, but I was going to be stronger this time. Plus, I needed this closure. I needed to tell Kevin to his face that we were over. I needed to take control of my life or I was always going to feel powerless around him.

The sound of a truck driving past drew my attention as I waited for the front door to open. I squinted in the dim evening light to make out what looked like a black truck. I wondered if it was Boone but shook my head. I needed to stop thinking that Boone was going to show up. I needed to get him out of my mind, or I was going to go mad.

Boone wasn't the only guy in Harmony who drove a black truck. For all I knew, he was long gone from this small town. Even though I regretted how I left things with him, my life was a mess, and the last thing I wanted to do was drag him into it. He deserved to find happiness with a woman who wasn't pregnant with her soon-to-be ex-husband's baby.

Just thinking those words made my stomach lurch.

My life was in shambles.

I turned my focus back to the door and knocked again. I peered through the clear glass sections to see if there was any life on the other side. I contemplated texting Kevin to let him know I was standing outside, but before I could reach for my purse, I saw his head pop out from another room.

I waved as he walked into the hallway and headed toward me. The sound of the lock disengaging filled the air around me, and I was met with the cool, conditioned air of his rental when he pulled the door open.

"Hey," he said as he moved to the side so I could enter.

Worry washed over me, but I pushed those thoughts aside as I stepped into the foyer and turned to smile at him. "Hey."

He glanced over at me as he shut the door. "Were you waiting long?"

I shook my head. "Not terribly long."

He stood in front of me, his gaze drifting over my body. "Good." He smiled down at me. "I hope you came hungry."

"Famished." I offered him a small smile, but my nerves were going haywire. It made my stomach feel like I was on a Tilt-A-Whirl. Eating was the farthest thing from my mind. But I didn't want to tell him that.

Suddenly he was stepping toward me. My entire body tensed as he lifted his arms and pulled me into a hug. I wanted to push him away. I wanted to step back and break his hold, but my body wasn't responding to the screaming in my head.

"I missed you," he whispered. His voice was deep and his gaze intentional as he held me close. Then he was leaning forward and his lips were inches from mine.

My body suddenly caught up with my mind, and I turned just in the nick of time. His lips landed firmly on my cheek. He pulled back, and I could feel his stare on me. I wasn't ready, so I took a moment, making sure to ground myself, before I turned to face him.

"We should talk," I said, ignoring the elephant that had wandered in and was now sitting squarely in the middle of the room.

Kevin's eyebrows were raised when I finally met his gaze. He paused before he nodded. "Yeah, I think we should." He glanced at his watch. "We have about ten minutes before the food will get here. Let's go sit in the living room."

He led and I followed as he walked from the foyer to the living room. He collapsed on an armchair that was perpendicular to the couch. He tipped his head back and closed his eyes, his chest visibly rising and falling with each breath.

Not sure where I should sit, I moved to the seat on the couch closest to him. I couldn't relax. The tension in the room was high, and I could feel it with every fiber of my being.

Such a stark contrast to how I felt with Boone. He made me feel at home, relaxed. I didn't have to fear when he was around. I missed that.

I could cut through the silence that surrounded us with a knife. I glanced around, wondering what to say. I wasn't sure how to say that I wanted a divorce. Or how to say that I was pregnant. My tongue felt like lead in my mouth. Even though I wanted to speak, it was as if I'd forgotten how. Nothing seemed to be registering with my mouth.

"How are things at the stor—"

"I'm pregnant."

Kevin stopped mid-sentence as he stared at me. I heard the words, but it took me a moment to realize that *I* had said them.

As if I needed to make sure that he heard them, I parted my lips and spoke them again. "I'm pregnant." There. It was out in the open now. He knew. I knew. My parents knew. There was no one else I needed to worry about. Everyone who needed to know about the pregnancy now knew.

The silence was sticky between us. Like the humidity

on a hot summer's evening. Kevin kept staring at me like he was trying to process what I'd said. Which was understandable. I had a near freakout in the bathroom when I found out, with Boone there to witness it.

"Is this a joke?" Kevin finally asked.

There was a bite to his tone that sent a shiver down my spine, but I brushed it off as shock instead of the anger that normally caused his sudden shifts.

"No," I whispered, offering him a smile with the hopes that it would help him calm down.

It didn't seem to work. Rage flashed in his gaze as he sat up straighter. Fear crept over me as I watched him stare down at me.

"Is this a ploy? A way to get me to stay with you?" His voice had gotten louder now.

This was a mistake. Coming here had been a mistake.

"Kevin, listen, I'm not lying to you." I raised my hands in a show of surrender, hoping that he would see I wasn't trying to rope him into anything.

"Who told you?" He narrowed his eyes as he jutted his forefinger in my direction.

"No one told me anything." I pulled back until the couch pressed into my back. I needed to get further away from him to protect myself and the baby. "I don't know what you're talking about."

He lunged forward. I yelped and brought my arms and legs in to protect myself. I expected a blow, but instead, he stood and started pacing.

My heart was pounding so hard, I could hear it in my ears. But seeing him put distance between us caused my adrenaline to dissipate, which left me shaking. I was grateful that he was on the other side of the room now.

"You have to know. Why else would you say you're pregnant?" Kevin was talking to himself now as he moved back and forth.

I wanted to jump in and reiterate that I didn't know what he was talking about, but I knew better. When Kevin was upset, the best thing I could do was remain out of sight, out of mind.

"Someone had to have seen me coming out of his office." He stopped and turned to face me. His gaze was dark as he pinned me with it. "You knew I filed for divorce."

I blinked as I processed his words. He was divorcing *me*? "Kevin, I had no idea. I just saw a divorce lawyer myself." I raised my hands once more to let him know that I was telling the truth.

His gaze didn't soften. If anything, it hardened even more. It was a look that I'd grown accustomed to. A look that said if I didn't do something, and quick, I was going to become the recipient of his anger.

"You planned this all along. The lies. You just want my money. You want to tie me to you." He stalked toward me. "You whore."

I pulled myself as far back on the couch as I could. "I don't want your money."

He shook his head. "You're lying. You know the courts will side with a poor pregnant woman."

"I'm not lying, Kevin." My heart was pounding so hard, I feared it would break free from my chest. The only way I knew I was going to get out of this was to stand my ground. I'd come here tonight to prove to myself that I had the strength to walk away, and that was what I was going to do.

I planted my feet on the ground in front of the couch. I wasn't going to let Kevin push me around. I was going to say my piece and leave. I was going to be the strong mother this baby deserved.

I moved to stand, but Kevin must have anticipated it. He crossed the space between us so that, when I straightened, he was towering over me.

"Where are you going?" he asked, his breath hot on my face.

I did everything I could to stand my ground. Even though the heat and the smell of his breath made my stomach heave. I wasn't going to show weakness. I was going to be strong.

"I'm leaving," I said, turning my gaze up to his so he knew that I was serious.

"No, you're not." He stepped closer, and we were almost touching.

"Kevin, I'm leaving," I repeated, my voice stern. I wasn't going to listen to what he had to say anymore. I'd done what I'd come here to do. I'd told him about the baby and that I was leaving him.

This was a chapter of my life that I was ready to turn the page on and move forward.

His hand wrapped around my upper arm. "I said no," he said as his fingers dug into my skin.

I winced but forced my voice to remain calm. "Let go of me." I reached up to push away his hand.

Suddenly, he threw me down onto the couch, the force taking the breath from my lungs. Fear surrounded me as I watched him lift his hand.

"You're not leaving!" he bellowed as he brought his hand down. I saw stars before I realized what had happened. My ears were ringing from the impact of his hand on my face.

He hit me. *Again.*

When my mind finally cleared, I curled my body to the side to protect myself from another blow. "Kevin!" I screamed, but that was muted by the sound of the front door slamming open.

I turned to see Boone barrel into the room. He glanced at me, cowering on the couch, and crossed the space between us. He shoved Kevin to the side before he knelt down in front of me. My purse appeared as he shoved it into my hands.

"Go," he said, his gaze desperate as he studied me. "Get in your car and drive home. Right. Now."

Suddenly, Kevin's hands were on Boone's shoulder, and Boone was thrown to the side. I scrambled to stand, wanting to help him, but Boone had stabilized himself and confronted Kevin before I could think.

The sound of a fist hitting skull made bile rise up in my throat. I turned, desperate to make sure it hadn't been Boone who had been hit.

It wasn't. He was shaking his hand, and Kevin was pitched forward, cupping his face.

"Go, Juniper," Boone said as he positioned his body between me and Kevin.

Not wanting to distract him, I nodded, shoved my purse strap up onto my shoulder, and hurried out the front door and down the stairs. I didn't stop until I pulled into my parents' driveway. I closed my eyes as my breath turned ragged. I could still see the way Kevin stalked toward Boone as I shoved my car into reverse and backed out of the driveway at Kevin's rental.

I couldn't shake the worry that Kevin had hurt Boone. I needed to know that he was okay.

A knock on the driver's window had me screaming and clutching my heart. I pinched my lips shut when I saw Mom peering in at me.

"Juniper?" Mom asked. Her gaze raked over my face, and I watched as her expression fell. Suddenly, the door was being yanked open, and Mom leaned in so she could get a better look at me. "Dear lord," she whispered as she reached forward and touched my swollen cheek. She tipped my chin so she could get a better look at my busted lip.

"Get out," she demanded as she stepped to the side.

My entire body was shaking now. "Someone needs to go back," I murmured as Mom wrapped her arm around my waist and pressed me to her side. I let her walk me away from my car for a moment before I stopped. "Mom! Are you listening to me? I have to go back. Boone needs me." I moved to push her hand away so I could break free.

"Juniper, you need to go to the hospital." She kept her arm wrapped around me as she started to lead me to her car.

"No. No, Mom." Tears were flowing now. Boone had done so much to protect me this last week. I couldn't walk away from him now.

"You can't go back there. I'll call the sheriff on the way to the hospital. I'll tell them what happened. But you need to get checked out." We were standing next to the passenger door of her car. Mom's fingers were wrapped around the door handle.

All I could do was shake my head and cry.

"Juniper, you need to make sure the baby is okay. Boone can take care of himself. He's strong." She'd turned her body so she was staring at me now. Each hand gripped my upper arms as she held my gaze. "You have to think of the baby now. Please."

I stared at her, trying to process what she was saying. And then, slowly, I began to nod. "Okay," I whispered.

Mom looked hopeful. "Okay?"

"Okay. But you're calling the sheriff on the way."

Mom pulled open the door, and I collapsed on the front

seat. "Of course," she said as she shut my door and hurried around the hood to the driver's side.

She stuck the key into the ignition, and the engine roared to life. I closed my eyes and tried to relax as she drove the familiar streets to Harmony Medical Center. I listened to her voice as she talked to the deputy sheriff. She relayed what had happened and the address of Kevin's rental. Then she thanked the deputy before hanging up the phone.

A few seconds later, her voice drew my attention. "Juniper?"

"Mm-hm?" I opened my eyes to see her face illuminated by the red light we were stopped at.

"The sheriff is going over to Kevin's place. He's going to take things from here." She glanced over at me. "Boone will be okay."

My throat felt crackly as I swallowed. My emotions rose up in my chest as tears pricked my eyes once more. All I could do was close them, or the dam inside of me would break and I was going to be unconsolable.

I had Boone all wrong. I'd allowed my fear of Kevin to cloud my judgement when I yelled at Boone. When I'd accused him of lying and manipulating me for his own gain.

From the look on Kevin's face when he saw Boone enter the living room, one thing was for sure. Boone did not work for Kevin, because Kevin *hated* Boone.

I'd run off the first man who had been there to protect me. If I ever got the chance to apologize to Boone, I would.

That man deserved my eternal gratitude, and I was willing to give it to him.

Problem was, I doubted he wanted it.

To him, I must be this emotional and fickle woman who jumped to the wrong conclusion every time. My life was a mess, and I doubted he wanted to be the man to help me sort it out.

No, Boone was going to leave at the first chance he got. And the truth was, I didn't blame him. I'd leave me, too.

24

JUNIPER

SWEET TEA &
SOUTHERN GENTLEMAN

I didn't feel better about Boone and what may or may not be happening over at Kevin's house when I walked into Harmony Medical Center. I waited anxiously next to Mom while she checked me in.

I couldn't shake Boone from my mind as the nurse led us from the check-in desk to one of the back rooms so she could take my vitals. I tried to stop worrying about him as I was brought to a bed where they used an ultrasound machine to check on the baby.

There was a brief moment when all the world around me faded away as the nurse pointed out the heartbeat in the tiny little bean inside of me. She informed me that I was about ten weeks along and that my morning sickness should die down soon.

But once the wand was no longer pressed to my stomach

and the machine had been turned off, thoughts of Boone came flooding back.

I was worried about his safety. I'd never seen Kevin this bad. He was not going to take lightly a man coming in to interfere with what he was doing to his wife. I'd already witnessed the contempt he had for Boone when he walked into my parents' house a couple days ago. I couldn't imagine how enraged he must have been when he saw Boone barge into his rental and stand between us.

I knew Boone was strong. I just feared what Kevin would do when he realized I was never coming back.

I also worried about the deputy sheriff. Would Boone be able to accurately describe what had gone on? That he was protecting me? I didn't want him to suffer consequences when I was the one who'd willing walked into Kevin's house, thinking that he'd changed.

He hadn't changed, and he was never going to.

I closed my eyes and leaned my head back on the hospital pillow Mom had situated behind me. She was currently scouring the hospital for some food and a drink. My stomach was tied into knots, but I knew if I didn't eat soon, the nausea would hit and I'd be making friends with the toilet bowl.

I focused on relaxing my muscles. My body felt as if it were sinking into the mattress. I was anxious and tired at the same time. It was an exhausting combo.

A soft knock on the door had me opening my eyes. I glanced over, expecting to see a nurse walking in, but instead I was met with a deputy sheriff. He had a notepad in one hand and a pen in the other. He turned as if he were about to leave, so I called out to stop him. "Hi."

He paused and glanced over his shoulder. "I didn't mean to wake you."

I shook my head as I pressed my hands against the mattress and pushed myself up until I was sitting. "It's okay. I wasn't asleep, just resting my eyes."

He nodded as he turned and then took a few steps toward me. "I'm here to ask you a few questions."

"I figured." I reached over and turned down the TV that Mom had turned on to give me some background noise. Then I set the remote on the side table and glanced over at him. "Okay."

He asked me some basic questions about what had happened. He let me know that he didn't want to push me past what I was comfortable with, but I just waved off his concern. I was ready for Kevin to face consequences for his actions. I was ready to take charge of my safety. I needed to for the baby.

If Kevin was going to treat me like a punching bag, he was going to suffer the repercussions. It was time someone held a Proctor's feet to the fire.

I recounted the evening, but I paused before I mentioned Boone. I wanted to know where he was before I talked about his involvement in the situation. So, I ended the story with Kevin hitting me.

The deputy was busy writing down my last statement. I

studied him, wondering how I could ask about Boone without raising suspicion. The deputy took a moment to read over his notes before he glanced up at me. "And Boone Grimes? What's your involvement with him?"

I stared down at my hands. What *was* my involvement with him? Who was he to me? Who was I to him? How did he know where I was going to be? Had that been his truck I saw passing by? Why hadn't he left town? I'd been so awful to him. Anyone else would have split and never looked back.

I sighed as I glanced up. I doubted the deputy had any answers to those questions. I would probably never get the answers to those questions. The best thing I could do was come to Boone's defense. He'd put himself in a bad situation to help me. It was only right that I return the favor.

"He's my friend," I said, hating that I'd treated him the way I did. "He must have been passing by and heard our fight. He came in to protect me. Kevin..." I paused, my voice cracking from the pain I'd lived with for so long.

The deputy drew his eyebrows together. "It's okay. Take your time."

I nodded in an effort to thank him for his words. I pinched my lips together until the wave of pain washing through my chest had subsided. I took in a deep breath. "I'm not sure what he would have done to me if Boone hadn't come in."

The deputy sheriff was quiet while he finished writing my statement. Then he clicked his pen and slipped it into his front pocket. He flipped the cover of his notepad closed and turned his attention to me. "Thank you for answering my questions." He gave me a small smile before he turned to head out the door.

"Excuse me," I called out.

He stopped and turned. "Yeah?"

I swallowed, unsure of how to ask this question. So I decided the direct way was the best. "Is Boone okay?"

The deputy nodded. "He's okay. He was pinning down Kevin when we got there. We offered him medical attention, but he denied it." He gave me a soft nod. "You have a good friend there."

Tears pricked my eyes. He was a good friend. The best of friends. I was an idiot for even thinking he could work for Kevin.

I swallowed against the emotions in my throat. "And Kevin?"

The deputy slipped his notepad in his front pocket next to his pen so he could fold his arms. "He's been arrested." He gave me a stern look like he wanted me to listen. "He won't be able to hurt you again."

I nodded. That was the hope. But Kevin was a Proctor. They had a way of getting out of things. "Thanks," was all I could say.

The deputy nodded and then left, closing the hospital door behind him. I lay back against the bed and closed my eyes, taking in slow, deep breaths. Kevin was locked up. Boone had walked away from the scene. I should be happy, but I wasn't.

I wanted to thank Boone for being there, and I feared that I wasn't going to get the chance.

Mom came in with an armful of vending machine food. We ate and talked until I yawned, and she tsked me for letting her talk so long. She threw away the garbage, tucked me in, and kissed me on the cheek. She would be back tomorrow morning to be with me until I was discharged.

I nodded as I settled back against the pillow and closed my eyes. I wasn't sure how much time passed before I heard the latch on my door release. I peeked over and saw the shadow of a man enter the room. He approached me. My heart was pounding with fear that it was Kevin, coming back to finish what he'd started.

I stilled myself, hoping he'd leave, but in the soft glow of the moonlight, I saw Boone's face as he peered down at me.

"Boone?" I asked as I pushed my hands against the mattress so I could sit up.

He stepped back as if I'd startled him. "I didn't mean to wake you up."

I found the remote attached to my bed and turned a light on. My entire body froze when I took in his face. His eyebrow had been split open. His cheek was bruised, and his lip was fat. He turned his face away from me when my gaze lingered too long.

"I'm so sorry," I whispered.

He shook his head. "I'm fine." Then he chuckled. "You should see the other guy." He slammed his mouth shut as if he'd just realized what he said. "I'm so sorry."

I shook my head. "Don't be. Kevin's an ass. I was a fool to think that he was someone I could have an intelligent conversation with."

Boone studied me for a moment. My heart trilled as he held my gaze. I'd been so wrong about this man, and I wanted him to know that.

"Boone—"

"How's the—"

We both stopped talking at the same time. He studied me before he waved his hand as if to let me continue.

"You first," I replied. I wasn't sure how he felt about me —if he felt anything. I didn't want to ruin our friendship by asking for more. And I didn't want to tie him down to this small town if he wanted to leave. I was scared.

He smiled at me before his gaze drifted down to my stomach. "Is the baby okay?" he asked, his voice going deep and protective.

There were so many things I wanted to say, but all I could do was nod. "It's okay." I offered him a small smile. "I'm ten weeks along."

He raised his eyebrows before he winced and brought his hand up to gingerly touch his split brow. "Congrats."

"Thanks."

Silence fell between us. He glanced around the room and then back at me. "And you? Are you okay?"

I nodded. "I'm okay."

His gaze drifted to the side of my face that Kevin had struck. It lingered there for a moment before he cursed under his breath and dropped his gaze to the ground. He fisted his hand as he shook his head. "I should have come in earlier."

"It's not your fault. I'm just glad you came in when you did."

He studied me before he glanced out the hospital window. "Still..." He was quiet for a moment. "I should go."

I raised my eyebrows. "Really?" I didn't want him to go. I wanted him to stay. I wanted him to know exactly how I felt about him. That I trusted him. That I had been wrong to assume the worst of him.

"I never meant to stay this long." He gave me a half-hearted smile. "Harmony was never meant to be my home." He paused. "I don't belong here."

My heart broke. I'd known this about him, yet I'd fooled myself into thinking that Boone would change his mind. He was transient. There was nothing holding him here but painful memories. If I cared about him like I professed to, I'd let him go.

I'd let him find his happiness somewhere else *with* someone else. My life was complicated, and he deserved something better.

"Okay," was all I could muster. If I kept speaking, I would break down and beg him not to leave. That was the last thing I wanted to do. Boone should stay because he wanted to. Not because I'd guilted him.

"Okay," he replied as he studied me for a moment and then nodded. "Goodbye, Juniper," he whispered.

"Goodbye."

He gave me one last look before he turned and grabbed the door handle. The sound of the latch engaging filled the silent room. I sobbed as tears began to flow down my cheeks. I buried myself under the covers and cried.

I cried for my previous life. I cried for the person I used to be. I cried for the baby and the broken home I was bringing it into.

I cried for myself. I cried for the fear that coated my body at the thought of doing this all alone. Sure, I had my parents, but this was my choice. This was my baby.

I cried for my broken heart. I cried for losing a friend. Boone knew all my secrets. He saw me at my worst and still stuck around. I cried for the love I had for that man.

But most of all, I cried from the realization that I was never going to see him again. Boone had changed me, and I was never, ever going to be the same.

25

JUNIPER

Mom was at the hospital bright and early the next day. She stayed with me until I was discharged. I was grateful to get out, and I was also grateful that the hospital was certain the baby was okay. They recommended a few doctors locally and in the surrounding towns for me to go to for prenatal care.

Dad was at the store when we got home. Mom helped me to my room, even though I told her that I could handle it. She shook her head and held my hand as she walked me to the doorway and then lingered.

I finally declared that I was going to shower and that she didn't need to help me with it. She was reluctant but finally shut the door to give me some peace.

The shower felt so good even though my face was still sore from where Kevin hit me. I was ready to wash off the hospital and the memories of what had happened yesterday.

I was tired of crying. I was tired of the pain. I was ready to move forward into the fresh, new future. The only regrets I had involved Boone, but the image of him happily leaving Harmony was the only thing keeping me sane.

He was going to find his peace somewhere else, and I was happy for him.

Mom was on her computer when I walked into the kitchen. I was wearing a pair of faded shorts and a tank. My hair was damp and hung past my shoulders. I was fresh and clean, and I felt like a million bucks.

"What are you doing?" I asked as I made my way over to the cupboard and grabbed a glass, which I took to the sink to fill up.

Mom gave me a suspicious smile. "I'm looking at baby clothes."

"Ma," I said before I took a sip of water. "We don't even know if it's a boy or a girl." I couldn't help the smile that emerged. I was ready to start feeling excited about this baby.

"I know, I know. I just couldn't help myself." Her smile spread across her face. "I get to be a nana."

Her smile was contagious. "I know. I'm excited for you."

"Come look at what I picked out."

We looked at baby clothes for the next thirty minutes. I swatted her shoulder when she put a bunch of gender-neutral clothes into the cart and then proceeded to pay for them. She shushed me when I tried to protest, claiming it was her grandmotherly right to spoil the child.

I laughed as I settled back on the barstool next to her

and took another sip of water. Mom was quiet for a minute before she glanced over at me. "Have you heard from Boone?"

I thought about denying that I'd talked to him, but I was tired of hiding things from my parents. I was better off when I had their support. So I nodded. "He came to visit me last night."

Mom's eyes were wide when she turned her full attention to me. "He did?"

I nodded. "Yeah. He wanted to make sure I was okay and to say goodbye."

"Goodbye?"

That word felt like a dagger to my heart. "Yes."

Mom paused before she turned her attention to the counter in front of her. Then she glanced over at me. "I went to Boone yesterday."

It was my turn to feel confused. "You did?"

Mom nodded. "After you told me that you were going to talk to Kevin and there was nothing I could say to stop you, I went to him."

I blinked as I tried to digest what she was saying.

"I wanted him to protect you."

"Oh," I said as realization hit me. That's how Boone knew where I was.

"I'm so sorry, Juniper. I needed to know you were safe."

"So you sent Boone."

Mom nodded. "I went to Boone." She sighed. "He was sitting in the driveway of his mom's house. I'd never seen someone so lost. I don't know the history there, but that man is hurting."

Pieces of the puzzle started fitting together in my mind. After I kicked Boone out of my parents' house, he went to his mom's. If he came to say goodbye yesterday, that meant he had to be settling his mom's estate. He was facing a past that haunted him as much as my past haunted me. But instead of having a family to support him, Boone was alone.

"I need to go," I said as I pushed the barstool back and stood.

Mom looked confused. "Go? Go where?"

I glanced over at Mom as I rounded the counter and headed to grab my shoes by the front door.

"Juniper! Where are you going?" Mom asked as she followed after me.

"I need to go to Boone's mom's house. He's alone, and I need to be there for him." I grabbed my purse and fished around for my keys. "Please don't tell me not to go."

When Mom didn't respond right away, I glanced up to see her studying me with tears in her eyes. "Go," she whispered.

"Really?"

She nodded. "You and Boone were meant to find each other. If he needs you, you go."

I drew my eyebrows together as my mom's words percolated into my mind. Then I nodded. "Thank you," I said as I leaned forward and wrapped my arms around her. "I love you."

"I love you, too, sweetheart."

I pulled back and turned to grab the door handle.

"I'll text you the address."

I shot her a smile of thanks before I headed out onto the porch. She followed after me, lingering at the steps while I crossed the yard and pulled open the driver's door. Mom's text came in when I was heading down our road. I pressed the link, and my maps app opened up.

I drove until I got to the Harmony Cove community. His mom's house was a few streets down from the entrance. I recognized his truck when I turned down her street. My heart was pounding as I pulled in beside it and parked my car. I glanced to the front of the house to see that the front door was open, which meant he was inside.

I hurried out of the car, slamming the driver's door behind me. I headed up the sidewalk and up the stairs. As soon as I got to the front door, I peered inside. I didn't know what I was going to find there, I just knew I needed to find Boone.

I softly knocked on the open door and waited. "Boone?" I called out, not sure if it was overstepping to just walk in. When there was no answer, fear crept over me, so I stepped inside.

If he was in here alone, I was going to find him.

I passed by some pictures on the wall of a small boy. I could only assume that it was Boone. The woman in a few of them had his same dark hair and blue eyes. She was holding him close and smiling at the camera. My heart ached for the small boy in the pictures.

Had he seen his mother get abused at that young age?

Seeing Boone with his mother made me realize that if I hadn't stood up for myself now, I would have continued this vicious cycle. I needed to stop the abuse and keep Kevin away if I was going to give this baby a healthy life.

I didn't blame Boone's mother. In fact, I understood her. I just wished she had found the strength to walk away. To start over.

I got to the hallway that I assumed led to the bedrooms. Some of the doors were open, so I headed down it. The first door was the bathroom, but Boone wasn't there. The next room's door was closed, so I walked past it to the far bedroom. As I stepped up to the doorway, I paused when I saw Boone sitting on the floor.

Clothes and things were spread around him. He was clutching a blanket in his hands. I hated that he looked so alone. So lost. I couldn't stop myself as I headed into the room.

"Boone," I said as I crouched down next to him.

He glanced up at me, his eyes cloudy from pain and tears. He stared at me for a moment before he closed his eyes. "You're not here. I'm dreaming," he whispered as he tipped his head back down.

"No, Boone. It's me," I said as I moved to sit cross-legged next to him. I wrapped my arm around his shoulders and scooted in close.

That seemed to startle him out of his trance. He glanced over at me and blinked a few times. "Juniper?"

I nodded, tears pricking my eyes. This pregnancy was going to do me in. I felt like my emotions were constantly right at the surface. I was going to die of dehydration before I got to the second trimester if I kept crying this much.

Then he frowned. "What are you doing here? You should be in the hospital." His gaze drifted over to the handiwork Kevin had left on my face.

I shook my head. "They discharged me. I'm okay." I swallowed. "The baby's okay."

His gaze made its way back to mine, and he held it for a moment before he looked away. "Why are you here?"

He felt a million miles away even though he was sitting right next to me. "I didn't want you to be alone," I whispered.

He closed his eyes for a moment before he opened them again. "I'm always alone." He stared down at the fabric in front of him. "That's what I deserve."

I shook my head. I wasn't going to let Boone believe that anymore. He deserved to be happy just like I deserved to be happy. We were two lost souls, drifting in the night. All we needed was for one of us to reach out and grab the other.

I would be that person if that was what he needed.

"That's not true, Boone," I said as I bent forward to catch his gaze. "You deserve the world."

He didn't look over at me. Instead, he just shook his head. "No. I don't. You don't understand what I've done."

He paused as he stared at the blanket in front of him. "I failed her."

"You didn't fail her." I reached out and cupped his face with my hand. Then I slowly tilted his face, forcing him to meet my gaze. "You were just a kid." I held his gaze, hoping he could feel what I felt for him. "You are a good man. Your mom would be proud of you."

His eyes brimmed with tears as he stared at me.

He wasn't pulling back, so I was going to keep going. This was my chance. Boone was drowning, and I was going to do everything I could to reach out and grab ahold of him.

"Your mom loved you. My parents love you." I paused as I held his gaze. "I love you."

His entire body stilled as he stared at me. His gaze searched mine in a sort of frenzied way. I could see his doubt. Then he dropped his gaze. "Don't do that. I don't deserve your love."

I hated that he couldn't see what I saw. I slipped my hand from his chin as I reached up and gingerly touched the bruised and broken parts of his face. The wounds he got from protecting me. "I don't deserve you," I whispered.

My words had his gaze snapping back to mine. He stared at me, and I could see anger build up inside of him. "You deserve the world, Juniper. You're beautiful and funny. You're so full of life, and I'm..." His voice drifted off. "I'm dead," he finally whispered. "I can't pull you into my hell."

Tears were brimming my eyes now. I leaned forward and pressed my lips to his.

He stopped talking, and I could feel his gaze on me as I pulled back just enough so I could see his lips.

"Did you feel that?" I whispered, flicking my gaze up to his.

He nodded.

I leaned in, this time letting my lips linger on his for a few seconds before I pulled back once more. "What about that? Did you feel that?"

His gaze turned dark as he murmured, "Yes."

I flicked my gaze down to his lips once more before I sat back on my heels. "Then you're alive." I reached forward and rested my hand on his. "If you let me, I'll remind you that you're alive every single day for the rest of your life." I shook my head. "I won't let you die. I can't let you die. If you do, I don't know..." My voice cracked, and suddenly, his hand was covering mine, and he pulled me into his arms. He crushed me to his chest as he held me. His hand moved to my head as he cradled it against his shoulder.

"I love you, Juniper," he whispered, his warm breath tickling my skin. "I've loved you since the moment I saw you at the store and you thought I was stealing garbage." His lips found the hollows of my neck and he pressed a kiss to my skin. "All I've wanted to do was protect you even when that meant protecting you from me." He pulled back, his gaze meeting mine before it drifted to my lips.

I nodded, loving his words and willing him to keep going.

"I was lost, and you were a beacon of light, guiding me to safety." He reached up and cradled my cheek with his hand. His thumb gently brushed the broken part of my lip, and his entire body stilled. "I'm not the man you deserve, but I promise I will spend my entire life trying to become him if you let me."

I smiled at him as a tear rolled down my cheek. "Okay," I whispered.

His gaze met mine, and I leaned in, welcoming the kiss I could see he wanted to give me. He pulled me in, and I closed the gap. My lips met his, and this time, I was going to show him exactly how I felt.

Our lips. Our breath. Our bodies fell into unison. I rose up onto my knees and moved forward, straddling him as he sat on the floor. His hand moved to my back as he wrapped his arms around me and held me so tight that I feared I might not be able to breathe. He tipped his head back and my hair fell around us, caging us in.

The heat of our bodies and breath caused my head to swoon. His tongue teased my lips open, and I obeyed. I was meant to kiss Boone.

Never in my life had I felt so complete kissing someone as I did in this moment. Everything I experienced with Kevin paled in comparison to what I felt when I was with Boone.

I was attracted to him, of course. But my feelings went

above attraction. I felt safe. I felt protected. I felt like I was the only woman on this earth that mattered. When I was around him, I felt like could do anything. Boone never made me feel like I was there to serve him. Instead, we were a team. He loved me and I loved him.

That was all that mattered.

We kissed until Boone pulled back. He didn't let me go, he just studied me, his brows drawn together.

I frowned as I brushed my fingers across the worry lines on his face. "What?" I asked.

"Am I hurting the baby?"

I studied him. "No."

He looked sheepish. "Oh. I thought maybe I was holding you too hard."

I shook my head. "I don't think there's much you can do to hurt the baby." I climbed off his lap and stood in front of him. I turned to the side and patted my stomach. "See? I'm fine."

Boone was watching me, his gaze trained on my stomach. Then, slowly, he rose up until he was kneeling in front of me. His hands found my hips as he turned me until I was facing him.

His hands settled on my waist as he leaned in and kissed my baby bump. Once. Twice. Three times. Then he tipped his forehead until it was resting on my stomach. "I'm going to love you, little squirt," he whispered. Then he pulled back and glanced up at me. "Just like I love your momma."

My hands found the sides of his face. I pulled upward,

signaling to him what I wanted him to do. He stood up, his lips finding mine before he'd fully straightened.

I kissed him, this time more passionately and more frenzied than before. He wrapped one arm around me and backed me up until I was pressed against the wall. He used his other hand to steady himself as his lips crashed against mine.

Never had I felt so loved in my entire life. Boone was my person. The man I was meant to find. Sure, the road to get to him had been broken and rocky. There were times I'd wanted to give up. But I'm glad I kept moving forward.

And I was glad that his broken road led to me as well.

I was going to love Boone for the rest of my life. He was the man I wanted to tell everything to. He was the man I wanted as the father to my child, as my lover in my bed, and as my companion as we grew old together. I trusted him with everything, and now, I was trusting him with my heart.

I was finally home.

And with Boone, I would never be lost again.

26

ELLA

SWEET TEA & SOUTHERN GENTLEMAN

Sunday morning, I woke up in a foul mood. I wanted to say it was because it was down pouring. The sky was dark and rain was pelting my windows, but I knew better. Today, the newspaper was being released.

The article about the Proctors was going to be read by the entire town. But more importantly, it would be read by Asher.

I moaned as I covered my face with my arm. I didn't *want* to write the article. I didn't get satisfaction from being instrumental in the destruction of my best friend's business. I just had to hope the fallout for Asher wouldn't be that bad.

Three solid knocks on my door had me pulling my arm down and staring at the ceiling.

Or maybe it was going to be just as bad as I thought it would be.

The knocks came again. I sighed, pulling my blankets

from my body and climbing off the bed. I grabbed my robe and stuffed my arms into the sleeves as I made my way to the door. It was Asher. It had to be Asher. I had very few friends who would come to my apartment at six in the morning on a Sunday.

I rested my hands on the door handle and dead bolt as I sucked in my breath. I'd written the article, it was time I faced the consequences.

Asher was mid-knock when I flipped the dead bolt and turned the handle. His hand was swinging toward the door when I pulled it open. He widened his eyes when he saw me. I could see a mixture of emotions as he stared down at me. If I could sum up his expression in one word, it would be betrayal.

"Why did you write this?" he asked as he held up the paper crumpled in his hand.

I folded my arms across my chest, hating that I'd ever been put in this situation. By him. By Gloria. By the strange man outside of the newspaper. Why hadn't anyone else been brave enough to expose what was going on?

"Asher, I had to," I said, wishing I sounded more confident than I felt.

He frowned. "No, you didn't." He paused as he stared down at the paper. "This will ruin my business. If any of this is true, they will assume I was complicit with fraud."

Guilt washed over me. "I know, Asher. But they were cheating people out of their homes. You were too blind to see it." I swallowed as my emotions rose up in my throat, making it hard to speak. "I tried to tell you, but you just said to ignore it." I freed one of my hands so I could wave it around, there was so much anxiety coursing through me. "You were too busy making deals to listen."

His lips were parted as if he were preparing himself to speak, but as the last words left my lips, he stopped. "Is that what you think this was? That I was just in this for the money?"

I stared at him. "Well, isn't that true?"

He scoffed and shook his head. He pushed his hand through his hair before he scrubbed it down his face and sighed. "You don't get it, do you." He straightened. "I was doing it for you. I wanted you to see me as someone who could take care of you."

I furrowed my brow. "I can take care of myself."

He nodded. "I know. I guess…" Then he shook his head. "Never mind."

He turned to leave, but I didn't want our conversation to end this way. I didn't want our friendship to be over. So I reached out and rested my hand on his forearm. "Asher, wait. What did you guess?"

He froze, his gaze dropping down to my hand before he brought it up to meet mine. He studied me for a moment and then sighed.

"I did it for you, because…it's always been you."

I stared at him. What was he saying? Did he mean…*no*.

"Asher, I…" My brain wasn't producing the right words.

I didn't know what to say, and yet, I feared if I didn't say something, he would walk away and never look back.

"It's okay, Ella. I never expected you to return the sentiment." He pulled his arm back and used his other hand to press the paper into my open palm. "I just never thought this was how you truly felt about me."

He dipped his head and walked back out to the hallway of my apartment complex. He paused, and I stood there like an idiot, watching my best friend walk away from me and feeling powerless to stop him.

"Goodbye, Ella," he said as he held my gaze for a moment before he turned and walked down the hallway.

I watched him disappear into the elevator and lingered in my doorway long after the elevator doors had closed.

Now alone, I stared down at the newspaper in my hand. I'd known this article would hurt the Proctors, and I'd known that Asher would be affected by the debris. I guess I just hoped it wouldn't have this kind of natural-disaster effect on our friendship.

There had never been a situation we couldn't work through. We were friends first and foremost, and I thought we'd always stay that way no matter what.

Apparently, that wasn't the case.

What had I done?

27

WILLOW

SWEET TEA &
SOUTHERN GENTLEMAN

I sighed as I stared out at the new sign I'd had made, pressing my hand into my lower back and curving outward to lessen the stress that had built up in my spine. My lips tipped up into a smile as I admired the curvy lettering. The Sunny Side-Up Diner.

I was so excited to bring this place back to its former glory.

After my uncle Douglas took over this place, he'd changed it to The Harmony Island Diner, but as soon as he willed the place over to me, I changed it back.

This was what it should have always been.

I never thought I'd be in the situation I currently found myself in. I was a single mom from Dallas, TX, barely making ends meet. My ex, Harold, was a joke. As soon as Jasper was born, he split, claiming that the baby wasn't his and he always knew I was a tramp.

I didn't care enough to fight him for child support, and my Great-Uncle Douglas needed someone to help run the diner since his arthritis was acting up. I jumped on the opportunity, and when I got here, he informed me that if I worked hard, he'd gift me the place once he was ready to retire.

True to his word, he'd signed the papers over and walked away, giving his blessing and his condolences. Sure, I'd never owned a business before, but I was excited for the journey I was about to go on.

"Miss?" The voice of an elderly woman next to me drew my attention. She had her glass raised in the air and was using her other hand to get my attention. "Can I get a refill?" she asked as soon as my gaze met hers.

I set down the rag I was currently using to wipe a table and nodded. "Of course," I said as I grabbed her glass and glanced down at it. "Was this a Coke?"

"Diet Coke," she replied.

"That's right." I gave her a smile, and she did the same before she turned back to her conversation.

I made my way through the dining room and walked right past the hostess stand, where a man was waiting to be greeted. He was new to this island—I'd never seen him before. He was standing there in a suit and tie, looking annoyed.

"I'll be right with you," I called out over my shoulder as I hurried past him and over to the drink dispenser. I pressed the Diet Coke lever and waited for the glass to fill. Once I'd returned the drink to the customer, I brushed my hands down on my apron and made my way back to the front.

The man was still standing at the hostess stand when I approached. "Just one?" I asked as I grabbed a menu from the basket.

"I won't be eating here," he said.

I glanced up and met his dark brown eyes. There was a coolness to his gaze that sent a shiver down my spine. "Okay," I said as I set the menu back down. "What can I help you with?"

He glanced around the diner before he sighed. "I'm looking for Douglas Gentlesman."

"He's my great-uncle. What do you need with him?"

He glanced back at me. "Well, for starters, I want to talk to him about how he thought he could sell off the diner without speaking to me first."

"Speaking to you?" I repeated before I frowned, confusion filling my mind. "And who are you?"

He reached into his suit coat and pulled out a business card. He held it out for me, but when it became apparent I wasn't going to take it, he dropped it onto the hostess stand.

"I'm Cole Watkins." When I didn't react, he continued, "Nick Watkins was my father." I still had no idea who that was.

Cole blew out his breath as he shifted his weight. "The man who owns half this diner."

***

I hope you've enjoyed reading Harmony Island Gazette. Boone and Juniper were both broken and looking for some light. I'm so happy that they found it with each other. It was intense to explore their story, but I'm glad I did.

I'm excited to write a best friend to more story with Ella and Asher and dive deeper into Willow and the new man who's come to town and disrupted her lift.

Make sure you grab the next book in the Sweet Tea and a Southern Gentleman series, The Sunny Side-Up Diner to find out what happens next!

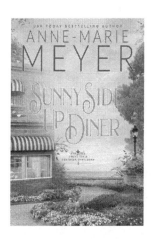

If you're wanting a bit more between Boone and Juniper, check out their SPICY or SWEET Bonus scene below.

Enjoy!

Harmony Island Gazette SPICY scene: HERE or scan below

Harmony Island Gazette SWEET scene: HERE or scan below

Want more Red Stiletto Bookclub Romances?? Head on over and grab you next read HERE.

For a full reading order of Anne-Marie's books, you can find them HERE.

Or scan below:

Made in the USA
Monee, IL
12 August 2024

63714779R00171